CHOKE

A NOVEL

BRYAN MATTHESON

2011 Flipjacket Inc.

ISBN 978-0-9840242-0-9

Published in the USA by Flipjacket Inc.

Printed in the USA

www.flipjacket.com

cover design by Brad Walker
www.bradwalker.net

Evening, first Friday in December

It's a minute and a half into the match, and there's no way I should be down two points. Matt Sorenson couldn't out-wrestle my grandma. Either the ref's blind or he's never read a rulebook in his life. Either way, I'm getting screwed.

We lock arms, my left and his right, heads next to each other. I've got a grip on his left wrist. It's all going quick, but not quick enough for Sorenson to keep his mouth shut.

"C'mon. At least *try!*" he hisses.

I know he's just trying to make me lose my cool, but I can't calm myself. I lunge at his chest, grabbing his leg for the take-down. I know as I do it's a half-second too early, I'm too far away to make it work.

My palm slips, rubbing along his leg instead of hooking around it. He shifts sideways and I'm rolling over his left hip. It's happening just like it had to, because there's no way it could *not* happen once I committed to the bad attack.

My left shoulder hits the mat and I roll to my stomach. I scramble to get my knees under me, and push up with my arms.

His hands knock my elbows down and he sprawls over me.

His hand grips my wrist. He's got me in a hammerlock, cranking my arm behind my back. But he's pushing it higher. Higher than he's allowed.

It hurts so bad I almost scream. I try to twist away, but he's holding tight. If he cranks a few inches higher my arm'll be spaghetti.

The ref's gotta stop this soon!

But the ref's on the other side of us, can't see what Sorenson's doing. He doesn't seem in a hurry to get a better view, either.

Coach is shouting now, pointing at me.

The ref shifts over for a closer look. But Sorenson lets go and wraps an arm under my neck. He shoves my face hard into the mat, and I'm hit by the stink of sweat and bleach.

"Eat it!" He spits the words at me.

The ref holds up two fingers. "Near-fall!" And I'm down four points.

Coach leans forward, almost stepping on the mat.

"That's bull –" he yells, even as Sorenson and I are getting to our feet.

The ref turns on Coach, holds his arm out sideways, hand in a fist. The sign for coach misconduct.

"Watch it," he growls.

Coach grabs the back of his own neck in frustration, so hard I can hear the slap of his palm on skin. His body's tightened up like he's been tazed. Me, Sorenson and the ref stand there a long couple of seconds, waiting for him to blow up. But he chokes back whatever he was about to say and steps back.

We get into starting position. I'm so mad my whole body's shaking. The anger's balled up in my throat, just fighting to get out somehow.

Sorenson's mouth twists into a cocky grin. I'm halfway to smashing it through the back of his skull with my fist.

Instead, I shoot at him again. Only this time, I get my hands behind both legs and the grip is tight. My legs shove upward, launching him into the air. He grabs at my shoulders, my head, whatever. I feel my hair getting yanked and his fingers rip the skin on my neck but it doesn't matter. I drive my shoulder down on his chest and slam him onto his back. I'm on him, flattened out, all 170 pounds of me laying flat across him.

I count in my head. *One-Two-Three.*

He bucks up but it's too late. He's pinned. It's over, and he knows it.

There's cheering from the stands. I roll off him and jump up.

But the ref holds up an arm and points three fingers in the air. Three points. No pin.

The gym's flooded by a wave of *boos* from the stands.

I can't believe it. "Are you blind?!"

He glares at me.

"What'd you say, son?"

"He was pinned!" I'm screaming now.

He glares, like he's ready to blow.

"Get back into neutral position, son!"

I step toward him.

"No way! I had him. A moron could see it!"

He sticks his arms straight out. "Unsportsmanlike conduct!"

I just about jump at him. My fists are twitching at my side, bunched into cannon balls.

Coach's voice stops me.

"Just get back to it, Ross! Pin him again and it'll be over!"

7

The crowd's screaming, swearing at the ref. His face goes redder, but he bites his lip, gets into a standing crouch, and looks from me to Sorenson and back at me again.

"Neutral position!"

I shake my head, get rid of the anger and control myself.

Sorenson just smirks.

The adrenalin's kicked in now. I shoot him again, and he backpedals two, three steps. I'm shoving all my weight into his stomach, my right hand behind his leg. Then he's slamming into the mat again.

I'm on him, one arm looped under his arm and around his back, the other behind his neck, hands locked together. He isn't getting away this time, no matter what.

The palm of his hand rams up against the underside of my chin, shoving my head back. It's straining my neck, hard, but I barely feel it.

Coach is yelling and the ref turns away to argue back. Seems I'm all of a sudden invisible.

Sorenson's hand slips out from under my chin and flails.

No way you're shaking me, I think.

But his thumb catches my eye. The sting rips into me.

Just like that, I'm twelve again and I'm on the basement floor with Ricky on top of me, mashing a mostly-empty taco chip bag into my face, scraping at my eye like steel wool. His buddy Mac's laughing his stupid head off. Mom's not home so I'm on my own. I'm trying to get away but Ricky's six years older and eighty pounds heavier and he isn't letting me move. I'm screaming at him, screaming at him to stop. But he won't.

I'm back in the ring, half-blind. Sorenson's squirming away.

"Nice try," he says, like it's funny.

That's it.

I lean back. The ref's looking our way again, and I sneer at him, thinking, *You wanna see unsportsmanlike? Watch this!*

I shift up on my knees, then throw my whole body's weight down on him. My elbow crunches against Sorenson's nose and cheek. It probably hurts me somewhere but I'm not feeling it. I'm not feeling anything at all.

His scream hits my ear like a siren. A few drops of blood spatter on the mat.

I jump up. He's rolling and his hands are covering his face. I almost kick him in the chest but hold back because there's no reason to. He's already done.

Coach rushes forward and grabs me, pulling hard, half-throwing me so I stumble away.

The ref's screaming, pointing at the locker room door. I don't hear any of it. I barely feel his hands shove into my chest.

I turn away. He grabs at my arm, but I shake him off.

My hand snags my duffel bag and jacket from the floor between Derek and Spence. They look away. My team mates are the only people not staring at me right now.

I slam the double doors open so hard they hit the walls in the hallway and I have to skip ahead before they bounce back and hit me in the face. The crash of metal door hitting concrete walls echoes around the gym like twin shotgun blasts.

I head down the hall, shrugging my arms into the jacket sleeves. Stop by the trophy case, get a half-reflection of myself. Brown wavy hair plastered to my head with sweat, green eyes rimmed red with anger, three long finger-scratches running down the side of my neck. Inside is the team trophy we won last year. The one we won't win this year.

9

I hold myself back from punching the glass and keep going down the hall. I back into the exit door so it swings open.

My feet hit the pavement, reminding me I haven't put my boots on yet. The winter cold stings my lungs, but I can't slow my breathing. My chest is pumping in and out, my heart still slamming inside my chest, and I head home.

Monday afternoon, 1:15

I'm trying to keep my balance walking on the top of the berm where the grader piled gray gravelly snow over the side-walk. The early storm left the town a mess. In a town like Ross-lyn in the middle of nowhere, Minnesota, you're lucky if they clear the roads, let alone the sidewalks.

My foot snags on a lump of snow that's frozen to the side-walk and I stumble forward. I have to put my hand on the ground in front of me so I don't land on my face. Not quite the lightening-fast reaction time you'd expect from a wrestler.

Except you're not a wrestler anymore, I remind myself.

The last couple of hours are stuck in my head, playing over and over. I figured the whole day would suck when I got up this morning, and it turned out pretty much like I knew it would. The kids'd had all week-end to talk about how I tore open some guy's face so bad he bled all over the mat. All day, they looked at me like a car accident you drive by, where your stomach turns but you have to watch it anyway.

Everyone but the team. None of them would say a word. There was no way they'd have anything to do with me after pull-ing a stupid move like I did on Sorenson. I was invisible to them.

First thing, they intercommed me to the office. Every head in the class turned to look at me like I was a spectator sport. Meyers gave me a nod toward the door, like she already knew I'd get pulled out. They probably told all the teachers about me before class. I pushed up to my feet and walked to the door. A couple of guys held their hands out for a palm slap along the way. I gave it to them and grinned, acting cooler than I felt.

I got to the hallway and stalled. Something wouldn't let me go to the office.

I walked over to my locker and sank to the floor, and slammed my head against the thin gray metal. I knew what'd happen. Coach and the principal and probably someone from the district would sit me down and point out stuff we all knew anyway. Then I'd get suspended from the team, and probably from school too.

I might as well have gone home but I couldn't make myself do that either. So I sat there like a useless lump of dog crap, with my back against the vents on the metal locker door and my butt bruising on the hard concrete floor.

A half hour later, I heard footstep slaps echoing from down the hall. Then Coach came around the corner. When he got close he gave a snort and flipped his head back down the hall.

"My office."

We walked into the gym and to the office on the left, in the corner past the bleachers. He pointed at an old wood chair with twenty years of graffiti scratched into it but I stood behind it. He sat back on his old tan metal desk. He didn't waste any time getting to the point.

"Do you know where I was just now, LeClaire?"

I snorted.

"Vegas?"

He bit his lip like he was holding himself back.

"I was in Wachinson's office. He'd already got a call from the Superintendent and was ready to hang you by your heels. So for twenty minutes, I had to tell the principal in twenty different ways why he shouldn't kick you out of school for good. How it wasn't really fighting, since it was part of a wrestling match— you know, tempers flare, it's all part of any sport. I told him how he should let you off with a week's suspension and an apology, even though I wasn't sure I should be sticking up for you. The whole time, I'm waiting for you so you can tell him your side of the story. Only, you didn't show up. You choked, kid. You lost your nerve and you choked."

I didn't need him shoving me into the ground even farther than I'd shoved myself all week-end. I kicked the chair in front of me.

"You saw the whole thing," I yelled. "You knew I was getting screwed, but you didn't do a thing. Where were you?"

"I was there screaming at you to win the match," he shot back. His face was getting redder by the second, but probably not as red as mine. "You should've been looking at me, not the ref."

What an idiot.

"You really think he would've let me win? I could've pinned Sorenson twenty times and the ref'd still give him the match. It was all over before I walked out onto the mat, and you know it."

Coach gave me a hard look.

"That match was over the second you let him get to you. It was over the second you gave up wrestling and played his game instead." He got this sad smile, like he was watching a puppy run in front of a school bus. "He got into your head because you let him get in your head, Ross. Instead of trusting me, you took care of it your own way. Now I can't go to the league and challenge the loss. I can't get that lousy ref disciplined. I can't point out that he's been best friends with Matt Sorenson's dad since they were in high school together. The only thing they care about right now is that some sixteen-year-old punk smashed another wrestler in the face and could've got the school district sued."

I started to say something smart-ass back at him, but Coach interrupted.

"So instead of clearing you and putting the whole thing behind us, I have to suspend you and watch the team's chances for a division title go down the toilet."

I looked down at my feet, studying the dirty almost-white linoleum tile. There was nothing I could say to that, because he was right, it was all true. Sorenson was a jerk for sure, but I was a bigger one. I knew it and so did Coach. The entire school and half the town knew it by now.

"You're a great wrestler," he said quietly. "Were since the first day I saw you, that scrawny six-year-old kid. You could've won state again this year, and you know it. You'd probably even get a college scholarship if you could just keep your nose clean. But you keep losing your temper. Last year it was that kid from Fosmark. In training it was Derek. Now this."

He stopped for a second. I looked up at the clock, wondering when I could get out of there.

"I like you a lot, Ross, but my hands are tied. You're out for the year. And Wachinson doesn't want you back in the school for the rest of the week."

I winced. Getting kicked off the team was pretty much what I'd expected. But even so, hearing it out loud from Coach felt like someone shoved a crowbar straight into my gut. If I couldn't wrestle, how would I keep in shape until next year? Who would I hang around with in the mean time? There was a pretty slim chance the team would let me anywhere near them at this point.

Coach gave me that quiet hard look again. He put his hand on my shoulder. I winced at first. But it wasn't like the hand on the shoulder I used to get from Ricky, the one that left a blotchy blue bruise I had to make sure Mom didn't see, because if she did I'd get it from Ricky again, only worse the second time. It was the opposite of that.

"There's something wrong with you," Coach finally said.

No kidding, I thought. Out loud, I said, "What do you mean?"

He puffed a breath out of his round cheeks.

"You're angry."

"No, really?" I shot back.

"I mean, deep in there"—he pointed at my chest—"you got a lot of crud bottled up." He put his hand under my chin and made me look him in the eye. I almost pulled away but something about Coach made me stay there.

"But something tells me you're not going to talk about it, are you?"

I gave him a blank stare back. He dropped his hand, leaned back to sit on his desk, and let out a sigh.

"You had better leave now."

He didn't say it like he was mad. Just like it was a fact neither of us could do anything about.

Before I could go, he added, "But if you ever want to talk this through, you come by and we'll talk, any time. I mean it, Ross. Any time."

That was four hours ago. And it's all I've been thinking about since.

Monday afternoon, 1:35

I wince at the cold going down the back of my neck. My ears and fingers feel like there's needles stuck in them. The eyelashes are freezing my eyelids shut, so I rub them hard and almost trip again. It's not supposed to be this cold a week before Thanksgiving.

I've been wandering around town for an hour but it feels more like three. There isn't much to do in the middle of a Monday afternoon in a town of thirty-five thousand. But I can't go home until Mom leaves for work.

If I was close to the drug store or JC Penny or something I'd go in and warm up. But where I'm at now there's nothing but a machine shop with a forty-year-old one-ton truck in front of it, a couple of storage sheds that look like they used to be red, and the old grain elevator that's one stiff wind away from being a pile of firewood. Three blocks from here is the part of town where the paint's flaking and the lawns are more weeds than grass and half the cars are up on blocks on the driveway. Our apartment may be a dump but at least it's close to houses you'd actually want to live in.

A flat-bed diesel pickup roars past me a bit too fast but that's about the only sound. No one but me is stupid enough to be out here when it's this cold.

I stop and hug myself and stamp my feet. Should've worn boots.

There's music—Johnny Cash or something just as bad,

15

muffled like it's coming through a wall. I turn around to look at the tin-sided old shop with a dented gray door. A little wood sign's screwed onto it.

Top Form Gym. Fighters Welcome.

I pull my hand back into my jacket sleeve and grip the round steel doorknob, pull the door open and step inside.

It's warm. Smells like pine disinfectant and fresh paint, mostly. A little sweat stink, too, but not bad.

I look around. The concrete floor has cracks as wide as my wrist and fifty years' worth of motor oil stains. There's new white paint on the plywood walls, but it can't hide the spots where pancake-sized sections have flaked off.

The place is crammed with worn-out stuff that looks like it's from a church garage sale. Blue wrestling mats rubbed white at the edges, an old red weight bench, dented iron weights and a bar. To the left, a long canvas punching bag with more duct tape than canvas, and one of those little boxing bags that hangs stiff from the ceiling. Some boxing pads are in the corner beside the portable stereo that's blasting the crappy music. To the right is a nine-sided cage that looks like it's made from the left-overs of three others someone found at the landfill.

At the far end of the room, a guy's putting up a poster. It's got a Hispanic dude in red shorts shooting a straight kick right at the camera, with "live to fight" in big red letters underneath.

The guy steps back and tilts his head like he's seeing if the poster's hung right. He shrugs and turns to me. He's an inch or two shorter than me, maybe 180 pounds and half-bald, and thick. The veins in his arms stretch like cables over his tight muscles and his neck's as thick as his quads.

He walks over to the stereo and turns it off. The silence

makes the place feel all of a sudden empty.

He folds his arms across his chest and runs his eyes from the top of my head down to my scuffed sneakers. I feel small, stupid, like a little kid.

"Uh ... you train fighters?"

He points at the door.

"That's what the sign says."

I look back at the poster of the Hispanic guy kicking. He's got on thin red gloves with the fingers cut off. Then the wrestling mat. The punching bags. The cage.

"Mixed martial arts, right?"

He shrugs.

"If that's what you want."

I've watched the MMA pros. They have a boxing coach, a wrestling coach, usually a Brazilian jiu jitsu coach. Probably muy Thai and a couple others, too.

"How many more guys you got coaching here?"

"None."

I almost laugh.

"You're good at everything?"

If he's annoyed he doesn't show it. He just looks me straight in the eye.

"Good enough for you."

My guts pinch. I'm a varsity wrestler and have thrown plenty of punches in way too many fights. And spent half my life surviving kick-boxing matches at home.

"You think so?" I shoot back.

He flips his head toward the mats. "Care to find out?"

I look from the mats to his cast-iron arms and neck and the scar under his left eye.

17

"No thanks."

We stand there eying each other. I'm getting more awkward by the second. If he is, he's not showing it.

"Right," he says. "Well, I've got things to do."

He turns and takes a step toward a few more posters half-rolled up on the floor.

"Okay. Well, I'll see you, then," I say, meaning, *If I see you in the grocery store, I'll be sure to head down the next aisle before you catch sight of me.*

"Yup," he says. He's already picked up another poster and a roll of tape and walking toward the wall.

I step outside and check the time. It's almost three. Mom'll be gone to work by now.

I pull my hands into my sleeves, crouch my head as far into my shoulders as I can, and head home.

Thursday afternoon, 3:00

For three days now I've done nothing much but lie on the couch going squirrelly, picking out the patched nail holes on the wall and wondering when we'll get curtains that didn't come from a garage sale. I've eaten everything in the house with any salt on it. Could really go for a beer but I usually score it from Spence, who gets it from his uncle. And I can't call him now, since I ignored two calls and three texts from him over the last couple of days. Just thinking about him or anyone from the team makes me feel like crap.

Of course, Mom knew about the suspension a half hour after they sent me home Monday. When she got home from work that night, she looked like someone had sucked all the blood out of her. I wish she'd lit into me but instead she sank to the couch with her head in her hands and half-mumbled to herself about her second son being irresponsible and a bully just like his brother. Then she looked up, crying, and asked why I didn't tell her about the wrestling match on Friday night already. I just sat there and took it. There wasn't much to say anyway, because she was right on all of it.

Then she went out Tuesday morning and came home with two bags of groceries and another bag full of schoolwork.

"That should keep you busy," she mumbled, as she dumped the bag of schoolwork on my lap before going to the little hole we call the kitchen to put away groceries. She hasn't looked me in the eye since she gave me the guilt trip the night before. I can guess why. Back when we had a decent house to live in, one with real wood cabinets and a fridge that didn't sound like it had smoker's cough, Dad used to sit on this same green couch from the minute he got home after work until he went out to the bar at eight. Sometimes when I got up in the morning he'd be sprawled across it, still dressed in the clothes from the night before. The mornings that he *did* come home, that is.

Two days later, I still haven't flipped open a text book.

I could hardly sleep last night, my legs twitched so bad. I've worked out every day for four months and now with the break, my body doesn't know what to do with itself. I went out for a run this morning but it was so cold my lungs felt like they were being scraped with steel wool, so I didn't get far.

All the time 'til now Ricky's been in the back of my mind. That picture of him kicking me in the side of the head just won't go away.

It doesn't take long to push the furniture out from the middle of the living room. I bounce light on my feet and give a couple of kicks at the air where Ricky's head would be if he was standing there. I can feel my foot making contact with the top of his neck where it meets his skull, and see his head snap sideways, and him falling down. Then a couple more, and a couple more, until I'm out of breath and my leg is cement.

The anger's still busting out of me, so I head into Mom's room to the body-length mirror screwed to the back of the door. I try to remember the training scenes from Rocky—throw a few punches at the mirror, look mean, connect with an uppercut and then a jab. But the guy in the mirror doesn't look anything like a boxer—just a sixteen-year-old wrestler trying to act tough. All I know how to do is throw down with some guy who ticks me off, which is more about charging him and hammering on his face than any kind of boxing.

My body aches to train, to burn off the anger somehow.

I head back to the kitchen for a glass of water, take a sip and look around. The ground-floor apartment is a glorified prison cell. Two bedrooms, a tiny eating area and a living room with barely space for a couch and the old recliner from Grandma's basement. The patio door leads out to a space with maybe four feet between the apartment and the cracked brown fence boards. When Mom tried to do aerobics for a couple of weeks last year she had to shove all the furniture into the corners around the table just so she could stretch sideways. Even if I could get hold of some kind of equipment there'd be no room to train.

I could always go back to the freak at the Top Form gym.

No way am I that desperate. MMA's great to watch, sure. But the kids around here who do it are losers. When they first

20

get into it, they talk all cool about it for a month or two but then one day they show up at school with a black eye or gashed forehead, and that's it. Every one of them chokes at the first sight of blood and none of them ever mentions MMA again.

That evening

I give one last painful turn at the curved hook that's screwed into the ceiling. My thumb and finger ache like the bones are bruised. My shoulders and neck are tight from wrenching on the thing while I was half-crouched between the chair and the ceiling. The stud in the ceiling must be made of rock. It didn't help that I picked up the longest screw hook I could find. Wouldn't want the whole thing to pull out and bring half the ceiling with it.

I got the idea while I was laying on my back on the bed after a hundred sit-ups and push-ups and jumping jacks. Coach would be proud.

Well, maybe not.

There it was, up above me. The almost-white popcorn ceiling that didn't quite cover up the lines where the pieces of drywall met. Then it came to me.

All those edges meet at wooden studs, probably rafters. The studs'd *have* to be pretty strong. All I'd have to do was get one of those screw-in hooks into the ceiling and hang a big canvas punching bag from it.

Then I pictured the thing hanging there in the middle of the room.

No way mom wouldn't notice it.

But I figured out I could just take the bag off the hook when

I wasn't using it, and shove it in the closet. Mom never goes in there anyway. With any luck, she'd never find out.

I went to the back of my closet and fished out the old tall duffel bag, soft tough black canvas with a hole on the end, and a rope sewn in to tie it closed. It used to hold baseball equipment from when Dad coached little league baseball one season. Well, only half a season. That was the summer he split.

After he quit, we never got a call about that bag full of gear. When we moved out of the house the next spring, Ricky sold most of it at a garage sale for beer money and since we were broke by then, we gave the few balls and a bat that were left as birthday gifts to our friends. The bag was all that stayed. It was too small, but it'd have to do until I could scrounge up a real punching bag somewhere.

I took the bag with me to Miller's Hardware and bought the long screw-in hook. On the way there I almost ran into Erin Magnuson and a couple of her friends. I took a quick right down a side street but not before she called out. I pretended not to hear. I knew her since grade school but she's not the kind who'd do anything remotely bad like open up a gash in a guy's face, and I'm embarrassed.

Coming back I went through the industrial area where I found an empty lot with a pile of dirt. It would hopefully be close enough to sand to make good filler. It was frozen, though, hard as rock. My nails are cracked and the skin on my fingertips are worn raw from scraping it up. I filled the duffel bag most of the way, tied it shut, and lifted it on my shoulder. It was good to have to grunt a little after a week on the couch.

I stand back and look at the screw in the ceiling and the bag on the floor. It should work.

I bunch the top of the bag up in my left hand, reach my right hand under the bag, and struggle upright. I sway a bit, shift my left leg over so the bag's up against the middle of my body.

I step my left leg onto the chair, then push up off the floor with my right, but as I reach full height I have to pull my head down sideways so it doesn't bang into the ceiling, which I do anyway. Then I'm off-balance, falling, landing on my chest with the bag under me. The landing makes a huge thud and shakes the room.

The slam of the front door snaps my head up.

From the hall: "Ross, is something wrong?"

Mom! Crap!

I grab the top of the bag with both hands and yank it toward the closet.

"What on earth are you doing?" She's in the doorway, hands on her hips. Even with make-up on, the wrinkles around her eyes make her seem ten years older than she is.

I can feel how guilty I look. "I thought you were working 'til eleven."

Jeez. That's about the stupidest thing to say.

"They let me off early."

She eyeballs me standing there stooped over, the drawstring in my hand. She looks around the room while I try to come up with a good lie to get her off my back. Her eye catches the hook in the ceiling. She looks back at the duffel bag and me and I wince.

"Oh, no. You are *not* hanging that thing up there. No way."

"Why not?" Which, again, is not the smartest thing to say. She'll give me half a dozen reasons why not.

"Ross, what are you thinking? If they find out what you're

23

doing, they'll kick us out and probably keep our damage deposit. Then what will we do? Where will we find another place where we can actually afford the rent? We'll be out on the street. Did that thought even occur to you once while you were pulling this stunt?"

I've got nothing to say to that.

"Take it down," she orders quietly.

"No."

"Take it down," she says again, even quieter this time. The anger's drained out of her face and she looks pale and a little stooped. I remember when she had that pretty smile and her eyes always sparkled green. Her hair was dark brown and wavy, too, not gray and limp like now. I know if I hold out a minute or two longer she'll melt onto the couch and cry all night until the anti-depressants kick in.

I take it down.

Friday morning, 7:15

The phone's ringing. My head starts to clear and I can feel my eyelids starting to open. I turn toward the wall and dig my head under the pillow. The phone rings again. Mom's voice is barely there, muffled by my door. I turn to my stomach and pull the pillow around my ears. But it's too late, I'm awake.

Friday. Last day of my suspension.

I push myself sideways off the bed. My feet are under me. My head's still foggy, but my legs and stomach and back and arms are twitching, pulling me straight up. I think again about the punching bag and Mom coming in on me, and I swear under my breath. I really need a workout. Cold outside or not, I might have to go running this morning.

I stumble into the kitchen.

Across the counter at our little table, Mom's half-finished a piece of toast. She's dressed already and has make-up on. She smiles. I guess the little incident last night didn't set her back too bad.

"Good morning. You'll never guess who just called."

I grab a bowl, spoon and the box of Cheerios and bring them to the table. I don't even try to look interested.

"It was your brother. Ricky."

I almost drop the milk. My hands are shaking. It's amazing how quick the anger takes me over.

"Don't you want to know how he's doing?"

I give her a look with no expression at all. I don't care how he's doing, as long as he's doing it a thousand miles from here.

She waits, gives a hard stare.

"Fine," I say, and pour the Cheerios. "How's my ___" (I leave a gap of quiet for effect, making sure she knows what I'm not saying) "brother?"

She smiles like she doesn't catch the swear I'm hinting at.

"He's good. He loves school, and they love him. He told me that he took apart a whole car engine last week and put it back together, and it even runs."

"Hallelujah," I say, staring at my Cheerios.

She puts her hand on my chin and lifts it up.

"That *is* good news, Ross. You and you brother may have issues −"

"He's a prick and I hate him. That's the only issue."

She sighs. "You don't hate your brother. No matter what you

25

might be feeling right now, he's your brother and you should care what he's up to."

She leans back again, issue solved in her mind. "He says by the time he's done in August he'll be a certified mechanic. When he moves back, he can get a job in any shop he wants."

I almost gag. "He's moving back?"

He went to school in Georgia to get as far away from Rosslyn as he could. He couldn't afford the plane fare back to visit—at least that's what he told mom—so I figured he'd stay there when he graduated. *If* he graduated.

"Yes, he's coming back. And that's good news, in case you're wondering."

My brain's shut down. Without thinking about it, I push my chair back as I stand up, and it flips backward onto the floor with a crack that makes Mom jump. I grab the still-full bowl of Cheerios a little too hard and it almost flies out of my hand as milk slops out the side and onto the table. Mom twitches, reaches out to catch it, but I snatch it away, stalk into the kitchen and pretty much throw it in the sink.

I walk to the closet, yank out my jacket, and barely resist kicking the tipped-over chair as I step around it on the way to the door.

She looks shell-shocked. "Where are you going?"

I don't say anything back, because I don't know.

I head outside and throw the door closed behind me.

I'm walking fast, no idea where to. I'm so jacked up thinking about Ricky that it feels like my heart'll explode out of my chest. He'll be back in May, mister big shot mechanic here to make his mama proud. He'll walk in the door, give me that cocky grin and punch my arm, hard.

I play the scene over and over. And every time, I get madder.

He grins, he punches my arm. He grins, he punches my arm.

It feels helpless. I'm the little brother, the one who gets hit. It's what I do.

No way. Not again.

He'll grin and go to punch my arm. But then he won't be grinning anymore because there'll be a fist plastering his lips into his teeth. He'll fall back to the ground, his arms windmilling while he tries to figure out what just happened. When he stands up, I'll flatten him again. It'll happen the same a few times more until his face is swollen up like someone took a bat to it. Then when he stands up one last time, I'll kick him through the glass patio door, just for old time's sake.

I walk another block, clear my head. He's got forty pounds and an inch and a half on me, so it won't be so easy. He won't know it's coming, and that'll help. But it'll take more than that to take him down.

There's only one way I can think of to beat him.

Twenty minutes later

I lean into the door of the Top Form gym and bend over a bit to catch my breath. Running here was more exercise than I've had in a week. I drag in a few more breaths of stinging cold air before putting my hand on the door knob.

I stand there thinking whether to go in. Might be a waste of time. The guy seemed like a bit of a dick the first time.

I shiver and look around. All there is are old buildings, dirty snow and guys driving by in pick-ups, right arm draped over the top of the bench seat. Life in small-town Minnesota.

Aww, hell.

I yank the door opened and step in.

It smells worse than the other day. More sweat. It hits like a punch to the inside of my nose. I see why right away. A guy's on the weight bench, pumping what looks like two hundred pounds pretty hard. Two others are sparring in the ring with head gear and light MMA gloves, fingers pointing out the ends. The taller blonde-haired guy aims a leg kick waist-high, but the shorter Hispanic guy shoots him for a take-down, grabs a leg, and throws him on his back.

Without realizing it's happening, I'm hyped up, my heart beating harder. My hands twitch, ready to fly. I can feel my legs lifting the guy into the air and my body rotating left as he hits the ground.

Just as quick, the Hispanic guy's rotating right again, straddling the other guy, mounted. He brings fists down at the side of the guy's head, one after the other. The other guy tries to protect himself but it's pretty clear the littler guy's got him.

"Alright. Up!"

It's the coach. He's on the other side of the ring, so I just see him now.

The top kid rolls over and helps the other guy to his feet.

"Hey!" I yell, and step forward a bit.

The coach sees me.

"Again!" he barks at the two fighters, and they square off.

He walks up to me.

He gives me a bit of a smile. Not much of one, but more than I got the first time I came by.

"You're back," he says.

I'm a bit unnerved. Not sure I should even be here. And the guy's face hardly moves—he isn't smiling or frowning, just standing there. I get the idea if I don't say something back he'll just walk away like I'm not even here.

"Uh, yeah." I look around, trying to figure out what else to say, soaking in again how scruffy the whole place looks even with the new paint.

"How often do you train?" I ask.

He looks me over.

"How much can you handle?"

"I'm in wrestling three hours a day right now."

I don't mention that I actually *was* going three hours a day, up until I got kicked off the team a few days ago.

"And that's enough for you?"

"I ... uhhh ..." Why wouldn't that be enough? No wrestlers train more than three hours a day that I know of.

"Sure. Maybe," I say. "Whadda you think?"

He shrugs again.

"Depends where you want to get to."

I point to the guys sparring in the ring. Now the blonde guy has his hands looped behind the back of the Hispanic guy's neck, pulling him in and slamming knees into the kid's chest.

"How much do they train?"

"A few hours workout in the morning, another few training in the evening."

I gulp. My body hurts just thinking about going at it that hard.

"What if I can only do part of that time?"

"Up to you. I'm not your babysitter."

I stand there awkwardly again while he's not saying anything. Half of me is ready to walk out again.

"Uh ... so ... I was wondering ..."

"Yeah?"

"Could I ... "

"Want to give it a try?" he offers.

I breathe out, relieved he's not leaving me hanging anymore.

"Yeah. Yeah, that'd be great. How's it work?"

"What. Training?" He shrugs. "The first time you come in, you spar."

"With who?"

He grins. It's the first time he's done that.

"With whoever's around."

He puts his hands to his hips, like he's including himself in the "whoever."

The guy looks like he's made of rocks. Even though he's half-bald, I can tell now that he's probably no more than thirty years old. He's been around—has cauliflower ears and scar tissue over one eye. There's a green and red tattoo, looks like some kind of cross and banner, on the bicep poking out from his sleeve.

Yup, the guy's a beast. But it's alright. I haven't been scared since Ricky broke my arm in sixth grade. He got in so much trouble I knew he'd never go that far again. Anything less than a broken arm is just hurt, and I've found out plenty of times that hurt goes away.

Assuming, of course, that they don't break a guy's bones in this place.

"I'm ready now."

He looks me up and down. I'm still wearing my pajama bottoms and a t-shirt under the jacket.

"Alright," he says.

I start taking off my jacket and my hand goes to my pocket.

"Crap!"

He turns back.

"What?"

"I forgot my money." Twenty-six bucks might not get me far, but it's all the cash I have right now, and it's sitting on my dresser. "Can I pay you later?"

He gives his half-grin again.

"The first one's on me."

"What about after that?"

He shrugs, motions me back toward the cage.

"We'll talk about it then. *If* you come back."

I'm about to ask what he means by that but he interrupts me.

"Hey Frank!" he yells.

The guy who's been hitting the bag pulls off his boxing gloves and runs up to us. He's maybe six feet tall, two hundred pounds, wearing blue shorts and a stretched-out old gray shirt that's tight around arms and shoulders. He's got some muscle. His hair's part brown, part gray—looks about forty-five.

"Yeah, Gill?"

So *that's* the coach's name.

"Frank, this is ..." He looks at me, questioning.

"Ross," I say.

"Ross," he echoes. "Take him into the cage, would you?"

I take off my jacket and throw it into the corner, kick my shoes after it, and pull off my socks. Gill is already at the cage waiting.

"Here," he says as I walk up, and hands me a pair of red

gloves. They're puffed up on the back and top, not as big as boxing gloves, and the blue vinyl ends at the first knuckle so my fingers poke through. I'm barely done pulling them on and he slams a set of boxing headgear over my head, so rough it mashes my ears.

"Ouch!"

He doesn't apologize, just pushes down to make sure it's on tight. I've only worn headgear for a few minutes once, at a boxing demonstration at the fair. It feels claustrophobic, and I can't see to the sides too well without turning my head.

"That work?"

I nod, and he shoves me through the cage door. The guy Frankie is already in there, bashing his fists together and bobbing his head side-to-side while he hops lightly on his toes.

"Ready?" he says with a grin.

I nod. We step toward each other and circle a little. It's not the straight-on "screw-you" kind of street throw-down like when me and the guys go down the road to Linville and get in fights behind the gas station. This is more thoughtful. This guy's not some farm kid who just comes at you like a bull, I can tell already.

He steps forward, pops to the right a little, then quick as lightning gives me a shot to the face with his left. I'm not used to the gloves and they hit hard. I say a quiet thanks to the headgear, but it still jolts me bad.

I reset myself, square up with him again. He hops close. I give a wild right hook. He blocks it and nails me in the stomach.

The wind's gone for a second. I stagger backward and get my bearings again. He's on the other side of the ring, dancing side-to-side, loose and calm like it's no big deal.

We close in on each other. I fake a right at him, he ducks left, and I swing a left at his ear. He pulls his head back but my fist hits his chin, a decent shot. He steps back a bit.

"Nice one," he says, and grins.

Next thing I know, he's leaning in and jabbing at my face with his left hand. It connects. Twice. Then his right comes around and nails me in the ear.

I go down to one knee hard, and a shot of pain knifes through it. I take a breath and feel the rug burn where the skin scraped the canvas.

"Good one, Frankie!" the tall blonde guy shouts from the side of the ring. He's laughing like it's piñata time at a kid's birthday party.

Frankie raises his fists over his head like he's Rocky, grinning like it's all a big joke.

That's it!

I jump to my feet and charge him. He's surprised and stumbles back a step, and I'm on him. My left arm snakes around the back of his neck and pulls him forward, and I give him two hard shots to the front of his face with my right glove.

I can see how my blows are rocking his face, how his body tightens up as each shot connects, the spit flying out of his mouth.

Yes!

The glove's too bulky for my hand to keep hold of his neck, though, and he easily pushes me away.

Without thinking, I spit out "How's that feel?"

I lunge forward for another shot, pulling my hand back to tee off. It's a blur and my brain can't quite catch up with what's happening as his body spins around and then his right hand is

33

extended and comes flying around from behind him toward the side of my head. My hands go up to protect me—too late—and the back of his hand slams the side of my face like a baseball bat. I stagger to the left. His right fist comes around hard on my ear. Then my mind clouds and I don't even see what must be a left fist straight to my ribs.

I'm down on the ground, rolling to the side, my hands covering my face. He's not coming after me. I push myself to my feet and catch my breath, waiting for him to pounce.

His arms are down, though, and he's bouncing again.

"Again?" he says.

I shake my head to clear it.

"Sure," I say, and try to grin. Like I said, it's only hurt, and hurt goes away.

It's time to stop thinking like a boxer and go with what I know. I charge, slamming my shoulder under his chin. He goes down backwards, hard. I'm feeling the rush now—less thinking, more just doing.

"Oooh! That's gotta hurt, Frankie!" a voice shouts.

I lunge, ready to jump on him and bring down fists, but he rolls to the side and is back on his feet. It doesn't matter. I'm feeling mean, in the zone, ready to take him down again.

He drops his hands and smiles. Then in two little hops, he's popping his fists in my face—left-right-left—I hardly know what's happening—then I'm doubled over, my ribs smashed— my head's rocked to the right—to the left—then another shot to the gut—then my tailbone hits the mat and I'm rolling onto my back, lying flat.

By reflex I lift my knees up to protect myself but he's backed off. I lie there staring at the ceiling, at the dingy yellow fluorescent lights and old painted-over pipes running across it. It takes a minute til my head clears a little and I'm breathing normally again.

"That good enough, Gill?" Frankie asks.

I struggle back to my feet. The coach is standing at the side of the ring. He nods. "Come on out."

I step toward the cage door. He shakes his head.

"Not you."

He nods to the blonde guy who was laughing a minute ago.

"Your turn, Mick."

The guy nods okay.

I'm getting the picture now. These guys are going to beat the crap out of me, send me home crying, and then go out for beers afterward and have a laugh. I wonder how many other people get the first workout "on the house" and never come back for a second round.

No way.

I shake myself out. My arms and shoulders are feeling tight but my head has mostly cleared. I stretch it left and right. My neck's sore.

I look Mick over as he pulls his gloves on. He's pale, stringy—probably six-three, narrow shoulders. No bulging muscles, but tight—looks like he's about six per cent body fat. His floppy, wavy blonde hair makes him look like some kind of Norwegian beach bum. He's only got one tattoo as far as I can see—a guy in a viking helmet with a pointy beard, about three inches wide, on the left side of his chest.

He stretches his arms above his head, throws his elbows back behind his shoulders, windmills his arms a bit.

"Want the head gear?" Frankie asks, ready to throw it to him.

He waves his hand at Frankie. "Nope."

"Good to meet you, Ross," he says, like he means it. He talks loose and light, almost chirpy. Not much like a viking.

I give him a little nod. "You too."

He holds one hand toward me and steps forward. I do the same. We touch gloves and each step back.

He got out-wrestled pretty good by the Hispanic kid a few minutes ago. So that's what I'll do—take him to the ground. And then, as they say in MMA, do some ground-and-pound.

We circle each other. I've probably got fifteen pounds on him, at least. That'll make it easier to control him when we take it to the ground.

He does a bit of a dance, jumps forward lightly. I move back. He jumps forward another step. I lean forward, ready to shoot his legs, but his leg twitches and I retreat. He jumps forward again and aims a fist at me, that long arm coming at my face. I step back and raise my hands to cover my face. A little boxing 101, courtesy of Ricky.

Thwack! His shin slaps against the outside of my left leg so hard it sends me reeling off-balance to the right. It feels like I've been hit by a block of ice, sharp on my skin. Ricky used to kick like that, but he never had close to this much power.

He steps toward me again, aims that right leg at me, but I'm ready for it this time and catch hold of his ankle.

I'm feeling good now. Kickboxing, I can handle.

But he's pivoting on his left foot, pulling his leg out of my grip, whipping his body back toward me, his right fist coming right at my face. I lurch my body down to the right just in time, then quickly straighten up again to protect myself.

Just in time to see the elbow swinging around and into my

cheek. I stumble backward and get some distance.

"Say hello to muy Thai," he chips, grinning. He kisses one elbow, then the other. "Weapons of the gods."

I give a sarcastic smile and charge, swinging hard. Lightning fast he puts his leg straight and it connects with my gut. I stumble back. He comes forward, aims a right foot and I jump back to dodge it. But in a half-second he slides in close. A fist under the chin, then another, then he's gripping my head from behind and pulling it down. I swing my body down and to the right just as his knee grazes my left ear.

But the guy's super fast. He's aiming another right leg kick, I can see it, and this one's coming right at my head. Just in time, I stick up my arm to block it, but the impact sends me rolling sideways. I jump to my feet but he's on me, all fists and elbows and knees, pushing me backward, and it's all I can do to stay out of reach.

As I hit the ropes, he hops back a step and as I bounce forward again, he aims another kick—the left leg this time. My brain's having trouble keeping up with the pace but instinct takes over and I protect my head.

Only, that's not where the kick lands. Now the sharp smack is to the inside of my left thigh, just below the groin. I fall back, spinning to the right, trying to catch my balance.

"That's the way, Mick!" Frankie calls out.

"Take it to him!" someone else shouts. In the back of my head I realize it must be the Hispanic kid.

My four years of sparring with Ricky is coming back to me now—need to do what he did. Wait for the kick. Block with the leg. Then lean in with the heaviest punch I can.

Mick comes forward, and the kick comes again, and I block

37

it just like I planned, and my right hand comes around, heavy from the shoulder like I meant. At the same time his fist comes at my cheek but my punch is pulling me to the side and his gloves grazes my cheek as mine smacks square into him, part cheek, part nose. He falls back, puts his hand to the red patch that's swelling under his eye.

"Oooh! That's gotta feel good!" the kid shouts.

"Want the face gear now?" Frankie calls out.

Mick looks ticked off. He shakes his head and jumps forward. His shin is arcing at my head, so fast I barely catch it. I manage to duck in time for it to only graze me. But he pulls it back and lets it go again. My hand comes up to block it, but it's too hard and too fast and it cracks into my skull under the ear.

I fall to my right side, stunned. Somehow I manage to roll and stumble back to my feet, backpedaling until I'm against the rope, leaning back to catch my breath and hoping he doesn't press me again.

Through the fog of my brain, I hear Gill call out, "Hey, watch it, man!"

Good. At least he doesn't want me sent to the hospital. Hope Mick feels the same.

Mick grins. "Sorry, my man. The gods get out of control sometimes." He flicks one leg forward, then the other.

I shake out the cobwebs.

"No problem." But I don't mean it.

"Are you sure you want to go again?" he asks.

I don't say anything back, just walk back to the center of the ring, two hundred wrestling matches and a dozen street fights playing in the back of my mind.

"Okay," he shrugs, and moves up.

He jabs at me with his left but this time I lunge, nail my shoulder into his midsection, grab the back of his legs and let momentum do the rest. He slams down on his back, locks his arms under my pits and around my back, trying to trap my legs with his. But I've done a little too much wrestling for that to work. I lean forward, lift my legs over his, straddle his body, and slip my hands under his arms to break their lock around my back. I'm on him.

He should've worn the head gear.

I'm remembering Sorenson, feeling anger flood throw my head and into my fists. I take a good couple of shots at his head, then bring down an elbow. It glances off his cheek bone—not full force, but enough to hurt. He's flailing now, blocking most of my shots. I lean back, cue up, and bring down another round. He swings an elbow up at me that bounces my head back but it doesn't even slow me down.

"Defend yourself! Stay active!" Gill calls out.

"Nail him, kid!" Frankie shouts above him.

Three or four more swings, and he bucks his hips and slips sideways. I'm out of position and he twists himself up and out. I grab at his back but he elbows me in the chest and shoves off. I curse at myself for letting him escape.

I'm so exhausted I can barely stand now.

Mick gets an evil grin on his face. He steps forward and I tense myself to block that right leg again. Only he steps forward on it instead and before I can adjust, his fist cracks into my ribs. I curl over to protect it, but it's too late. Then a knee's heading up at my face. His hands are behind my head, pulling me down. I eat the knee and start to fall. He's still got hold of my head and his knee collides again. I manage to pull away, but he gives a roundhouse punch with his right hand instead. It rocks me to my right. I straighten. This time it's his right shin cracking against my left ribs. I recover and make a lame attempt to rush him again, but he backs away and I stumble forward. He dances on his toes, teeing up again.

"That's enough!" Gill shouts out.

Mick feints at me again and I flinch, but his hands drop to his sides and he grins. I stagger to my feet and he gives me a big hug, patting me on the head.

"Nice work," he says. I'm not sure if he means it or he's mocking me.

I step toward the cage door, pulling my gloves off. I can barely breath. Every move hurts my ribs. My head throbs and I wonder if I have a concussion.

The Hispanic kid is stepping through the open doorway to the cage, headgear and gloves already on. He looks at me with fake surprise.

"What, you're quitting already? But I haven't had my turn yet."

I sigh, shake my head and pull the gloves back on. I'm not sure how to go another round, but backing down isn't an option. I never did with Ricky.

"Not today, Gabe," Gill calls out. "He's had enough."

The guy shrugs. "Fine." He points a fist at me. "But I get first shot next time."

I pull my gloves off and open the cage door, trying not to fall as I step out onto the gym floor. Gill offers a hand, but I brush him off and manage to stay on my feet.

Gill punches me a good one on the arm. I try not to cry out. "Get your money's worth?"

I try to smile. "That's one way to put it."

He looks me up and down and gives a little laugh.

"You coming back?"

I look around the gym, and at the three guys who are already walking away. I'm replaying the fights, mad, thinking how to end it with them feeling as bad as I do right now.

I don't answer, because I'm not sure. I still haven't made up my mind as I step outside.

Twenty minutes later

I'm so tired and battered I barely make it in the door without collapsing. My shoulders feel like bunjee cords are pulling them together behind my back. My quads ache and my head feels like lead.

I try to shrug my jacket off with my arms straight down behind my back. Chest, arms, neck, thighs, quads all scream at me. As I twist to get the sleeves past my wrists, my ribs pinch and I almost cry out.

I'm hit with a whiff of sweat from my pits and the back of my shirt's soaked too. I'll have to wash my jacket at least once just to get the stink out.

All I want to do is sleep. I head down the hall toward my room. My stomach growls, sending me back to the kitchen with a groan.

There's four eggs left in the fridge and I crack all of them into a bowl and whip them up with a fork. Every flick of my wrist sends an electric shock up to my elbow.

I bend down to get the pan out of the cupboard—another painful move—and put it on the burner.

While it heats up I rummage through the fridge and pull out the bag of shredded cheese. Behind it is a little pack of beef slices so I pull those out, too. I'm not in training anymore, Coach isn't there to get on me about my diet. I've earned the calories.

While the eggs are cooking I cram half the pack of meat into my mouth.

I put my hands at my waist and try to arch my body sideways over my legs.

"Ho-ly!" I moan. It's more ache than I've felt in years. Those guys were brutal.

"What's wrong?"

I jolt upright and whip around. Mom's standing there, looking me over.

"What happened, Ross? Are you hurt?"

I groan. Getting into it with her is all I need right now.

"No, I'm not hurt. I'm fine."

She raises an eyebrow.

"Maybe I'm imagining things, but you don't seem fine."

I look past her, wishing there was an escape route to the hall.

A whiff of eggs frying reminds me and I turn to the pan and start flipping them around.

She walks up and puts her hand on my shoulder. I do my best not to wince.

"You look really worn out, Ross. Tell me what happened." Luckily there aren't any visible bruises—the worst are on my chest and left thigh.

I reach for the bag of cheese and dump some into the eggs.

"It's nothing. I'm just tired."

I grab the orange juice out of the fridge and hope she leaves so I can lean against the counter.

"What from? Where were you?"

Before I can think, it slips out.

"Training."

She pulls a glass out of the cupboard and passes it to me.

"What do you mean? You aren't allowed to train with the team anymore."

Crap! That's all I need, her figuring it out.

"Not training. Just exercising on my own. I went running. Can I eat now?"

She gives me a look that says she doesn't believe me.

I put the eggs on a plate and walk past her to the table. As I dig in, she starts making herself a lunch.

"Have you done your schoolwork?"

"A little," I mumble.

She stares at me until I look back.

"A little?"

"Alright. I'll do it this afternoon."

"There were a lot of books in that bag I brought home," she says. "Please, Ross, just do it. Please. Don't fall behind. If not for your own sake, then do it for me. You just got your average up to a 3.0 and it would crush me if you let it slide."

She puts her knife down and looks at me hard. "Wrestling's no guarantee of a college scholarship, you know. Especially now that you're off the team for a year. And you know I won't be able to pay for school."

"Yeah." I've heard that enough times from her by now. When's she going to leave?

She works on her sandwich a little more, puts it in a bag, looks at me and sighs again. I bend over my eggs and pretend not to notice.

43

It takes her a few more minutes to get everything together. I eat slowly, waiting for her to get out of here. Neither of us says anything. Finally she gets her jacket on and grabs the lunch and her purse. She comes over to me and I lift my forehead so she can kiss it.

"I'm gone until evening. Get that schoolwork done, please?"

"Yeah."

When she's gone, I groan back to my feet, put the plate in the sink and stagger to my room. I'll shower later.

Two minutes and I'm asleep.

Sunday evening, 9:20

I throw down the remote and push myself off the couch. At least I don't have to roll off like all day yesterday. I can't remember ever being this sore two days after a wrestling match.

There's no way I'm going back to that gym. It hurts to walk. It hurts to breathe. Those guys beat the crap out me. Pounded a sixteen-year-old kid into the ground. It's taken the past year and a half since Ricky left for me to get over those beatings. I don't need to get into that kind of abuse again.

It was bad enough being crippled all week-end. Having mom around peppering me with questions didn't add to the fun. I tried to make it look like everything was okay, like it didn't hurt to even think of moving, but there's no way she bought it. She saw me in that kind of shape for most of my first fifteen years.

It happened a few times a week, sometimes more. Dad would take me and Ricky downstairs to learn judo. He'd show us a move, then tell Ricky to practice on me, which meant using me as a living punching bag. If I so much as winced he'd call me Loretta and ask me what color panties I was wearing. Then after way too long he'd tell Ricky to stop and say it was my turn, which meant I'd take the best shot I could at Ricky and then he'd smack me in the ear. After a few minutes of that I'd usually just lunge at him, swinging my arms like I was trying to swim him to death. Which Dad thought was hilarious. I dreamed about smashing Dad into the ground almost as much as doing it to Ricky.

I'm not going back to that life again. No one's going to put me there. Not Ricky, and definitely not the guys from Top Form.

Monday morning, 8:10

The hallway's full of kids, but it thins a bit and I see Erin's long dark hair and red sweater. She's standing at her locker, alone. She looks up and sees me. Too late to turn away.

I feel my face heating up. It wasn't as bad as it could've been, showing up at school after the week's suspension. Seems like most of the world's moved on. And I don't care what most of them think anyway. But Erin's different. Somehow she matters.

I walk up, trying to think what to say. Luckily, she talks first.

"Hi, Ross. How're things?"

I try to look as cool as I can. "Good. You?"

"I saw you Thursday, out by the post office."

I scuff my foot on the floor a couple of times.

"Yeah. I was ... going to the drug store for some medicine for my mom. Didn't feel well."

45

She looks me in the face, concerned. "Oh, I'm sorry. Did she get better?"

"Uh, yeah, she's okay."

That was close.

"What'd you do all week?" she asks.

Crap. I can't tell her about going to Top Form. The whole idea sounds lame, like I was trying to be Bruce Lee or a professional wrestler.

"Nothing much."

"Did you get out much? Could you find anyone to hang around with? I hear the team's still a bit mad, other than maybe Spence. He asked a few days ago if I knew how you were doing."

She gives me the look she's always had—like she's curious, but she cares, too.

"How are you doing, really?"

"Good." It's the easy thing to say. She probably deserves more.

She looks at me closer. Her green eyes seem like they see right into me, like there's no point in lying.

"I've been worried about you."

"Me? Hey, I'm fine. I've been worse."

A clump of kids walk past us, talking, bumping us without noticing. A few look at me but I try to keep my eyes on the lockers so they don't stop to chat.

"Is it okay if I ask you something?" Erin asks.

I'm guessing it's about the wrestling match, which isn't even remotely okay, but I nod anyway.

"There's something I've been wondering." She speaks slowly, like she's trying to find the right words. "Why did you do it?"

There it goes. She doesn't have to say what 'it' is. I know.

And there's no good reason for bashing a guy's face in, even if he deserved it.

"Look, I already feel bad enough."

She blushes and shakes her head in frustration. When she does that, there's a little red spot at the back of her cheek that gets redder than the skin around it. It's always been there.

"Sorry, that didn't come out right at all. What I mean is, what's the reason? Honestly? What made you so mad that you had to punch a guy in the face?"

She pauses a few seconds, then figures out what she wants to say next. "I heard once that everyone does what they do for a reason. Even if the person doesn't realize what the reason is, it's there. They don't just do things out of the blue. I think that's true."

She stops talking. I don't know what to say, so I just look down the hall.

She says quietly, "I've known you long enough to know you're not a bad guy on the inside."

It's nice of her to say that, even though it isn't true. We've never talked about it, but she has to know how me and Spence and the guys go pick fights in Truman and Linville, for no good reason except we're bored and it feels good to punch guys in the face. Nice people don't do that kind of thing.

I look down at my jeans. They're worn and baggy in the wrong places. The oily stain on the left leg has been there so long I can't remember. And the shirt is stretched out at the bottom. It doesn't look as cool as I thought it did when I put it on this morning.

I look back up at her. She's turned away, like she's embarrassed.

"Th – thanks," I manage to mumble.

She turns back and smiles.

"You're welcome."

We just stand there, quiet. I shift my feet a little, try to remember if I brushed my teeth this morning. She pulls her long brown hair back behind her ear. She's got silver hoop earrings on.

Alexa walks up and stops beside us.

"Hey, Ross. Elbow all healed up?"

I bite my lip so I don't say something that'll get me kicked out of school for another week.

"I better go," I say.

Erin looks from Alexa to me.

"Yeah, me too." She puts her hand on my arm. It still hurts a little and I almost pull away but manage to keep it still. "I'll see you soon, okay?"

Then she gives me that quiet smile of hers as she walks away with Alexa. I'm too slow smiling back but I try to do it in time. I hope she noticed.

Thursday morning, 5:30

I can't believe I'm here, standing at the door to Top Form, ready to get hammered again.

I play it over in my head.

On the way out of third period Tuesday morning, Spence told me one of the guys had a new phone that was worth checking out. I knew what he really meant—they were ready to let me back in.

I wasn't that excited and was kind of watching if Erin would wander by but eventually I headed over to the wrestling room.

When I came in, Spence right away yelled, "Hey, guys! Elbows is back!"

Heads turned. Derek yelled out, "Elbows!" like I was a soldier returning from battle. A few others did the same, with "hey there" thrown in.

It took me a second. Then I imagined that elbow cracking into Sorenson's head.

Elbows. That's me.

They were mocking me. Or had they got over how I wrecked the chances of a team win, and were giving me some kind of street fighter cred? Maybe both.

Then they were getting into it like always, slamming each other on the shoulder, into the wall, calling each other names that generally involved body fluids. I started to get into it with them, make the same old jokes, but after a while I hung back. I'd been there so many times—hung out with half of them so long I couldn't remember not doing it. A few of us were wrestling together since I was six, the year Coach came to town and offered classes evenings and week-ends for extra cash.

But something happened that Friday evening two weeks ago, when I left the gym with Sorenson a bloody mess on the mat behind me. I don't know what, exactly. But I didn't feel like being in that wrestling room.

I managed to stick around until lunch was over and bump around with the guys in the hall until we got back to class. I didn't look for them after school, though.

By the next day, my body hardly hurt anymore, other than a huge charlie horse on my right quad with Mick's name written all over it. That's when my legs and shoulders started firing again, telling me to do something, make them work. I caught myself dreaming about fighting Mick again, and Frankie. If I was sharp and didn't lose my cool, I might be able to get in some decent shots next time. I swung my arms forward, fist out, a looping right meeting one of their faces. Then a knee, a left fist, a kick. I could just feel the impact in my mind.

So here I am, six in the morning, walking into Top Form.

The four of them are here—Mick, Frankie, Gabe, and closest to me, holding the pads for Gabe, is Gill. I walk up to him.

He puts down the pads. Gabe nods at me, walks over to the punching bag and starts hitting it one-two, one-two-three, one-two.

Gill eyes me.

"Back for more, huh? Ready for the rest of it?"

"What?"

"Hey Gabe," he calls. "Take off the gloves. He needs you," he says with a grin, gesturing at me.

"Get your jacket off and stretch a little if you need to," he tells me.

I can't believe he's throwing me into the ring with Gabe, too.

"You're serious?" I ask.

"Of course I'm serious. Mick, Frankie, now Gabe."

My arms and ribs can still feel the last beating.

"I'm just a kid, you know."

I feel like a loser saying it, but damn it, it's true.

Gill shrugs. "Not in here, you're not."

I'm not sure whether to slug the guy or walk out. Slugging would feel better but from the muscles in his arms and the way he holds himself, it might be the last punch I ever threw.

"What do you mean? You think you can treat me just like a bunch of guys who've been training for years?"

Gill eyes me coolly.

"I don't train martial artists—I train fighters," he says. "These guys moved here or drive an hour every day *because* it's so tough. They want to push themselves to the limit. That's the point. We're all here to become the best fighters we can be. Even Frankie over there"—he points at the older guy—"he'll probably never step into the cage for a real match, but when he's here, he's here to throw down. I don't care who you are or how old you are. If you want to be a fighter, you're welcome. But we're all equals, fight-wise. No special treatment. You fight or you don't last. It's up to you."

He nods at the door.

"I got three or four guys a week come in here saying they want to be a fighter. Most of them don't last. We're okay with that."

Then he walks back to Gabe and tells him to keep on the gloves, and he picks up the pads again.

I sit down against the wall. It's hot, but I don't take my jacket off.

Gabe's hitting those pads quick and hard. Gill's moving them up, down, side to side, and Gabe's not missing a shot. As he hits, he bobs high and low, dances back, forward, and smacking those pads the whole time. It looks like he could do it with his eyes closed, it's so natural. I'm getting tired just watching him, but it's been five minutes and he's not slowing down. Sweat's pouring off him but he snaps every punch.

Gill finally puts down the pads and walks over to hold the bag from behind. Gabe rests for a minute or so, then nods and starts doing kick and punch combinations, bobbing and shifting like before.

He looks over at me, then focuses on the bag again. After another couple of minutes he lets a bunch of high right kicks go one after the other, right beside Gill's head where Gill's holding the bag. Then he steps back, drops his hands, and unties the gloves with his teeth.

He looks at Gill, motions at me with his head. Gill shrugs like he doesn't know. Or care.

Gabe throws the gloves to the side, picks up two sets of headgear, and walks over to me.

"Hey. Let's do it, huh?" He motions to the cage.

The question hangs there. Every muscle in my body's telling me not to do it, but I know if I leave the gym right now I'll never come back. I can just see going back to the wrestling room, hanging out for the rest of the year, putting in time until I'm allowed back on the team next season.

Gabe throws the headgear onto my lap.

"C'mon," he says.

I realize my jacket's on the floor beside me. Must have taken it off at some point while Gabe was hitting the bag.

"We'll take it easy this time," he says.

"Yeah?"

"Yeah. Promise ya."

He holds out his hand and pulls me up, and we head for the cage.

Friday morning, 10:45

I'm sore again. Even worse than last time. I can barely focus on the back of Julie Watkins' head, and she's sitting only three feet in front of me. Every half minute my head's jolting forward and I wake up and Meyers is still droning on.

Gabe's idea of taking it easy wasn't the same as mine. He let me wrestle him, no problem. In fact, he didn't even try to stop me most of the time. It seemed like he actually *wanted* to take the fight to the ground. I found out why pretty quick. The first time I got on top of him, I got in one punch before he lifted up to jam his hip into my armpit and started spinning out. I'd stopped spin-outs a thousand times, and I put out my arm to the mat to stop him. Just like that, he'd hooked his arm around mine and was leaning into the back of my elbow. I could feel it starting to hyper-extend and panicked.

"I give! I give!" It felt lame, like I was a five-your-old giving up in a fight on the schoolyard.

He let go right away and stood up. I followed slowly.

"You don't have to yell if you don't want," he said. "Just tap me twice."

We did that a few more times. I'd take him down, and he'd somehow manage to wrap his body around me. One time he cranked my right arm behind my back. The next he had his leg over my left shoulder and was cranking my arm back until my shoulder screamed at me. Tap out. We went through it a half dozen more times and each one ended with me getting an arm or knee or ankle cranked until I was a half-second away from torn ligaments. Fighting it took all my energy, 'til I wanted to just quit and lie down for an hour.

Then I got a good sprawl on top of him and lifted up to give him a couple of shots. A second later his elbow was in my face, hitting me hard enough to leave a welt I hoped would be gone the next day. I finally managed to get seated on top of him and he looked surprised so I figured he was in trouble. I remembered how Ricky did it to me—a right, a left, back and forth against the side of the head and then when he covered up, a hammer fist to the face. But all of a sudden Gabe bucked, swung his body around and over me, and he was on top of me the same way. My arms were pinned. I bucked but couldn't move him. It was pretty clear he could've planted my head six inches into the mat if he wanted. But he got up. Let me go.

Then one last time, I watched for my opening and shot him again, a solid double-leg takedown. Right away, though, he propped himself up. I put my weight down on him but he looped his arm around my neck and reached under. I felt his grip tighten and I struggled back, but he clamped down even harder.

"Tap," he told me.

"No way," I croaked.

"Seriously, tap."

There was no way I was going to do that. All I could think of was how mad I was at this jackass for making it look like I hadn't wrestled a day in my life. I pulled away harder but it felt like a noose was tightening around my neck. I tried to push myself up to get a shot at his head or body or something.

The next thing I knew, I was lying on my back and Gabe was standing over me, putting down a hand to lift me up.

I shook my head to get my vision back.

"What happened?"

"You took a little nap."

I let him pull me up.

"Next time, tap out," Mick said from the other side of the cage fence.

Gabe slapped me on the back. "That's probably enough, don't you think?" I nodded and got up slowly, and stepped out of the cage. At least it was over, and I hadn't been battered from head to shin. I'd be able to walk tomorrow.

Then Gill ambled up from the other side of the room and shoved me back inside.

"My turn."

I hurt already just thinking about it.

Julie's shaking me, hissing "Wake up, Ross!"

"Mr. LeClaire!" Meyers calls out. "What was the location of General Custer's fort?"

"Uh..."

Alexis smirks at me. Derek whispers something to Martin and they laugh.

"The city and state. Where was Custer's fort?"

She waits a second but I'm still trying to clear my head.

"You don't have a clue, do you, Mr. LeClaire? I'd venture to guess you have not done a single scrap of homework in recent memory. Am I correct?"

"Just a sec," I say.

I think back five years. I was reading a book I'd got from those book sale magazines they send home with you a couple of times a year. Ricky was working his way through tenth grade for the second time. Across the room at the kitchen table, Mom was drilling him on the Civil War for his final exams while he paced the room. She kept coming back to the same questions over and over while he went on about not needing to know history anyway since automotive school didn't even look at your transcript.

He got another answer wrong and I must've snickered. "You think I'm stupid? Heh?" he yelled, and faked a lunge at me. "Go back and read your fairy tales, little girl." I walked to my room while Mom gave him the answer. After hearing her tell him four times over, it got drilled into my brain so deep I'd probably remember it when I was gumming my dinner in an old folks' home. His big battle was in Wyoming, but his fort was in …

"North Dakota?"

Meyers puts her hands on her hips.

"And what city in North Dakota?"

She looks annoyed, like she wants me to not know.

"Bismark."

She glares at me a second.

"Alright."

She keeps going on her lecture and Julie turns half way around.

"That was close!"

"Nice save!" Spence whispers across the aisle. He holds out his hand and I reach over and slap it. My shoulder tightens up immediately.

It was sparring with Gill that did it. In five minutes he showed me fifty ways to get past my hands or fake me out and plant fists and feet into me. The thing that really ticked me off was knowing he was toying with me. I'd take a swing and he'd block it and counter. Not enough for any permanent damage, but enough to leave bruises the size of pancakes. I'd kick, he'd block it and return the kick, only he'd actually make contact with his shin. Ricky always hit me with the foot. The shin was way worse.

Then I'd move forward to jab and he'd give me a body shot or kick the inside of my thigh. Those really hurt. After ten minutes of that I could barely stand and my punches were as limp as a rubber chicken.

When it was over he told me I did great. I couldn't tell if he was making fun of me or not, because he was grinning wide and I'd never seen him do that. Then the other guys slapped me on the back. It hurt my bruised muscles so bad I almost fell over, but it still felt good.

As I slowly managed to get my coat on, Gill said, "Next time we'll take it to the ground." I wondered if that was his way of saying I'd passed the test, I was part of the gym for real. Half of me hoped that wasn't what he meant, so I wouldn't have to come back for more punishment, but it still felt good, like I'd survived a battle.

An hour and a half later

Class is over and everyone's leaving as quick as they can. I hang back so I won't bump into any of them on the way out the door and pass out from the pain.

I push myself slowly out my chair and grab my binder.

"Hey there."

Erin's hung back too.

We walk to the door together.

"Are you okay?" she asks. "You seem pretty quiet these days."

"Yeah, I'm fine," I say back.

"Are you still hanging out with the wrestlers?"

"Not really."

We're walking down the hall now, heading for my locker without thinking.

"Good," she says. "Maybe there's hope for you yet."

I feel myself blush, but right away I get mad.

"What's that supposed to mean?"

"It's the wrestling," she says. "No offense, but it makes you guys so aggressive. You—I mean, most of the guys—they push their way around like they're pit bulls and the rest of us are Chihuahuas, only they're not. They're the same dumb guys we all knew since kindergarten."

Okay, she's right. But she doesn't get it—how good it feels to push yourself hard, take your feelings out on the mat, just you against the other guy.

"The worst part is, they look at girls like they're meat. It's disgusting."

I step back, getting mad now.

She stops walking and grips my wrist to stop me.

"I mean, most of them do. Treat girls that way. You don't do that, though, and you never have. You're a decent guy."

I can't tell her I want to learn how to kick a guy in the head with my shin and crank his arm behind his back until he can't take it anymore. I sure can't tell her my plan to take Ricky down when he comes back at the end of summer. Talk about aggression—I've got it running through my veins by the gallon.

Erin frowns. "Still, it must be hard on you to not be hanging around with those guys."

I shake my head.

"Not really."

She stares at me, hard. "Are you sure you're not even a little bothered by it? You've been really quiet lately."

My arm's starting to hurt holding my binder, so I switch it to the other other arm. Even that hurts my ribs and I stifle a groan.

"Yeah, I'm sure."

She looks me over, worried.

"You look exhausted. Are you having trouble sleeping? Are you still feeling bad about the ... the incident?"

I think about how I barely stayed awake after my bout with Gill yesterday and was passed out on my bed by eight.

"No, I'm sleeping fine."

"Then what?"

"Nothing. I'm telling you, nothing's wrong."

She sighs, and puts her hand on my shoulder.

"Listen, I have to do some research for that Civil War project Meyers gave us. Do you want to come? We could work on it together."

All I can think about is sleep.

"No, that's okay," I say back. "I'll work on it over Christmas."

She puts her hand on my arm and gives me that smile again.

"Just don't let yourself fall behind, okay?"

Friday night

I can't sleep. It's one in the morning, and I've been lying here staring at the ceiling for two hours. I'm so tired I can barely get myself out of bed to go to the bathroom. The beat-downs the Top Form guys gave me—they're going around in my head a hundred miles an hour. I can see the kicks, the punches, the submissions coming, the same ones over and over. Can't help obsessing over what I could've done, what I'll do next time.

Part of it was me not being ready. It was nothing like the fights in the schoolyard, the beatings we'd give each other in Spence's basement, the fights we'd pick with kids we didn't even know just for fun. Those were about rushing the guy, slamming into him, nailing him as hard as you could with fists, head-butting if you had to. And making sure him or his buddies didn't have a knife or beer bottle or baseball bat nearby.

I can plan it out now, at least a little, think through what to do next time I get into it with the Top Form guys. Mostly, though, I don't have a clue. Those submissions Gabe pulled were nasty. They came out of nowhere. And then the combinations—how all four of them would fake with one hand and connect with the other, then follow up with a brutal kick to the side of my leg or ribs. I just can't picture a way out of that.

My heart's hitting against my chest and thumping inside my head. I can't believe how they battered a sixteen-year-old kid. Can't believe a bunch of guys who are probably pros, or could be if they wanted, took it to a kid who's never stepped into the cage. Most of all, I can't believe I was that helpless, how slow and stupid it felt standing there taking the hits and tapping out on the ground.

Next time I'll do damage. I'll figure out how to get in there more. They may still win, but they won't walk away smiling this time.

Around 1:30, it hits me. Even though I can barely turn over without wincing in pain, I feel as alive now as when I won state last year. My body's wrecked but my mind's firing a hundred times a minute. Next time, I swear to myself. It'll be different next time.

Saturday morning, 10:30

Turns out there's a lot of stuff about MMA on the web. First I figure out which martial arts the guys used to beat me. Obviously, Mick and Gill used some boxing. Frankie especially nailed me with those fists. For an old guy, he's quick. But I'm younger and wrestling's taught me evasion techniques, lateral movement, that kind of thing, so at least it's a start.

Then muy Thai. A little digging on the encyclopedia site tells me it's from Thailand. They fight close-up—it's all elbows, hands, knees and feet. A few videos of muy Thai fights show the techniques Mick used to take me out. It's brutal—lightning fast, with the hammer-hard strikes from the elbows and the knees to the ribs. Worst of all were those feet and shins hitting my head and legs, over and over. Like getting hit by a bag full of concrete. Gill didn't use as much of the elbows and knees—more kick boxing, really—but I got the feeling he could've if he wanted to.

Then there' the Brazilian jiu jitsu Gabe pulled on me. I could wrestle him down, smother him, but just like that his legs were snaked around me and pulling my hips over and he'd rolled on top of me. Or he'd just stay there on the bottom and trap my arm or leg or shoulder with his. Either way, in a few seconds some part of my body was getting stretched out or twisted so my joints were hyper-extending and I knew I was a few seconds away from some kind of serious injury.

On the web, I also learn a couple other things I'm sure Gabe could've done that looked just as evil. I guess he was taking it easy on me, after all.

I watch a few instructional videos that walk through a bunch of the moves, but it's a little much to take in. There's a lot to learn.

That afternoon

Mom comes in and asks if I've been on the internet all day. I grunt, which she takes as a yes.

"What are you doing on there? Anything I should be worried about?"

I take my eyes off the screen, try to look sincere. "Just research."

She's not buying it.

"What kind of research? Are you behind in school? You're letting your grades slip. I know it. You are, right?"

Actually, the last few weeks my grades have fallen a little, but she doesn't need to know that. I couldn't handle her crying about it.

"They're training videos. That's all."

She gives a sad frown.

"It's wrestling, isn't it?"

"Yeah." Not *only* wrestling, but since wrestling's part of MMA, technically I'm not lying.

"You miss it, don't you?" she asks.

"A bit." I sigh so she'll believe I'm really shattered.

She comes over and ruffles my hair. I slip to a blank screen so she won't see the kickboxing match I've been watching.

"It's only a year, Ross. The season is over in a few months and then in a few more, school will be out, and you can train with them again in the summer. You'll have two more years to wrestle. Don't worry. I'm proud of you, though, for trying to keep up your skills."

I look up. "Thanks, Mom."

She stands beside me a little more, her arm around my shoulder, pulling me into her. I feel kind of bad lying to her. But the truth, that I'm learning how to pound guys into the mat any way I can, would probably freak her out. *Definitely* freak her out.

Sunday evening, 5:30

It's Christmas eve. It feels like there should be something special about it, but not in our house. It's just Mom and me and she's half burned out by life and still getting over a cold. Probably remembering when it was the four us, her and me and Dad and Ricky, and thinking it was so great, although it wasn't even close to okay, as far as I can remember.

We eat mac and cheese dinner. Mom makes small talk and I try to return the favor. I'm cleaning up the dishes when she comes out of her room in her nicest dress.

"What's up?" I ask.

"I'm going to church. You should come with me."

"Nah."

"You really should."

"What for?"

"It's Christmas Eve, Ross. You know that."

"So what?"

"You have to go to church on Christmas Eve."

"Why?"

Her face is getting redder. I push one step further.

"We never go to church. Why's today any different?"

Her hand jolts forward almost like she wants to hit me.

"Because it's Jesus' birthday. It *Christmas*, for Christ's sake." She realizes what she's just said and blushes.

63

I laugh. "Nice one. No thanks. I'll stick around here."

She slouches and sighs.

"And do what?"

I look around the room, asking myself the same question.

"I don't know. Stuff."

I spend a half hour flipping channels and another fifteen watching Brazilian jiu jitsu lessons on the internet. This'd be a good time to learn a few things. Instead, I go back to flipping channels.

That lasts about five seconds and I'm up pacing around the living room. I go to my bedroom and look up at the hook where I was going to hang the boxing bag. I think about trying it again. The old duffel bag's still in the closet. It wouldn't take that long to fill and hang it.

But that would be pushing Mom a little too far.

I go back to the couch, fall back into it, turn on the TV again, flip for a few minutes. There's nothing on TV on Christmas Eve. Maybe I should've gone to church with Mom. At least it would've got me out of the house.

I gotta talk to someone. I'm going batty sitting around here.

Erin. She's gotta be busy Christmas eve. Who knows? Maybe not. I flip channels a couple more minutes.

Ah, why not.

She answers on the fifth ring. It's a relief it wasn't her mom or even worse, her dad.

"Hey, Erin. It's Ross. What're you up to?"

"Oh, you know, just hanging around..." She sounds awkward. I hear noises in the background.

"You got something going on?"

She doesn't respond for a second. "Yeah, kind of. My older

brother and his wife are in from Seattle, and my Uncle Vic should be here in a few minutes."

A voice in the background yells "Erin! Did you stir the punch yet?"

My heart goes up my throat. I feel like throwing the phone across the room.

"Oh, jeez. I can't believe it. I – I'm sorry. I shouldn't have called."

She jumps right in. "No, no, that's alright, Ross, really. We're just sort of hanging around here. I've got a few minutes to talk before we get into the presents."

I hear Christmas carols in the background and a bunch of laughter. "Erin!" someone yells over top of it.

"Actually, Ross, I'd better –"

I'm the biggest idiot. What was I thinking, calling her on Christmas Eve?

"Yeah, yeah. Me too. Listen, sorry I bugged you. It was stupid. You have a good time."

"Okay, Ross. Listen, I'll call –"

But I don't hear what else she's saying because I've hung up.

I get up, pace around the room, throw a fist at the wall and pull back just in time so it doesn't make a dent.

I gotta get out of here.

I throw on my coat and runners and head outside.

My ears are frozen in less than a minute, but I'm not going back in there.

Ten minutes later I'm hammering on the door to Top Form. No answer. I bang again, yell "Hey! You in there?"

As if Gill would be here tonight. The guy's gotta have some kind of life outside the gym.

Wednesday afternoon, 2:30

There's a call coming in from Erin's number. It's the third time she's called since Monday. And texted twice. I don't answer. It's a pity call, I know it.

Top Form's closed. I hope it opens soon because this house is a prison.

Sunday morning, 10:20

Somewhere in the corner of my brain a doorbell's ringing.

Now someone's talking. I force my eyes open. The room's bright already. I must've slept in pretty good.

The door opens and Mom's head pokes in. "Get up, honey. Someone's here for you."

She leaves. I groan and turn my legs off the bed, stand and pull on a pair of jeans; then a t-shirt I've worn a couple of days now. I sniff my pits. Could be worse.

I come out and there's Erin, standing there looking nervous. *Crap! I should've known!* I resist the urge to smell my pits again.

Mom's not around. I look back down the hall and her door's closed.

"Good morning, Ross," she says.

I mumble something back and then try to smile. My eyes are still stuck half-shut. I stretch and shake my head to clear it.

She's wearing jeans and under her jacket, a tight green sweater that brings out her eyes. No makeup, but she doesn't need any. She looks up at my face and I picture my greasy bed-head hair and how one ear sticks out sideways, the one Dad used to call my shark fin.

I mumble something back and step into the little kitchen. I can still see her over the counter.

"Want some juice?" I ask, and grab a couple of glasses out of the cupboard.

"No thanks."

She steps closer so she's right on the other side of the counter.

I pull the carton out of the fridge and turn back around. She bites her lip and flips her hair behind her ear.

"Did your Christmas turn out alright?" she asks.

I pour the juice and put the carton down on the counter.

"Yeah, it was alright. Good." I breathe in and get a whiff of my own breath. She must be gagging from the stink of it but she doesn't let it show. I turn to the side a bit so she won't smell it as much. Plus then I don't have to look her in the eye. I take a swig of juice, hoping it'll wash some of the smell down my throat.

"Listen, I'm sorry I couldn't talk when you called the other night," she says. "It's just my whole family was there, my mom needed my help because we were about to –"

I swallow another mouthful of juice and wave my hand at her.

"Don't worry about it. If I had any family around, I'd have done the same thing." Even as it's coming out of my mouth, I hear how pathetic it sounds, like I'm an abandoned dog stuck in the pound.

"I called and texted," she says. I can't tell if she's hurt or worried. Either way, I look like a loser.

I feel my face getting hot.

"Yeah, sorry. I got busy and forgot to get back to you." Which sounds mean, like she isn't worth the time. *Idiot!*

"Oh. I just thought I'd see how you were doing."

"Yeah, well like I said, it's all cool so don't worry about it."

She leans over the counter and puts her hand on mine, looking hard into my face. I want to pull away but it feels good.

"Are you sure?"

Now I'm mad. At both of us—me for being a charity case, and her for making me sure I know it. I pull back.

"Look, I – there's a bunch of stuff I gotta get done." I kind of gesture around at nothing in particular. "You know, homework and ..."

She steps back too, looking down at the ground, maybe trying not to cry.

"Okay. Yeah, me too. I'm sorry I – sorry I woke you, Ross. I better go, huh?"

I don't make a move as she opens the door and goes outside without looking back at me.

Mom's door opens and she walks up to me. She cuffs me in the head.

"Dumb kid!"

First Monday in January, 6:30 in the morning

I haven't been up this early in months.

Why am I doing this? Every other kid in town is still asleep. And when their alarm finally goes off, they'll stand under a warm shower for ten minutes and slowly get used to the idea of starting school again.

But not me.

It's almost zero degrees and I'm out here in workout pants and a sweatshirt pushing a wheelbarrow with a few fifty-pound weights in it, through a foot of snow. My hands hurt so bad I can barely keep them wrapped around the handles.

It's not such hard work once I've got a little momentum going. But as soon as the wheel catches or my foot slips, I have to wrench the thing the other way with every muscle in my arms and shoulders and stomach and legs to keep it from tipping. And half the time I sink into the snow and the thing falls over anyway, and I have to start again.

Why are you even here? I ask myself.

I bite my lip. That's the same question I could tell Gill was wondering when I showed up this morning. He was all smiles when he finished whipping my ass the Friday before Christmas, but he sure looked surprised to see me a half hour ago.

Gabe's ten feet behind me, pushing his own wheelbarrow. I look back at him. He's a few inches shorter than me, maybe five-eight, probably a hundred sixty pounds. He's quieter than Mick, less intense. He has this easygoing way of shuffling around like nothing much is going on. You'd never know he was deadly quick once you got him into the cage.

"Pretty tough, huh?" I say.

He grins.

"It's not so bad."

You get the idea nothing seems too bad to him. Still, his wool hat has blotches of sweat coming through it and he's breathing pretty heavy.

I stop to catch my breath.

"How long you been coming to the gym?" I ask.

He keeps pushing his load past me. "Gill just opened it up in October," he says. "Before that, I was with him at his gym in Rochester for a year or so."

69

That's two and a half hours away, I think.

"You moved all the way here from Rochester?"

He pivots the handles around the front wheel, straining to keep the load upright, then heads back my way. I turn around with him.

"I ripped out of there as quick as I could get out of my lease, which was early November," he says between gasps for breath.

"Just to stay training with Gill?" I ask.

He stops and wipes his forehead with his sleeve.

"Got a better reason?"

He pushes forward again. I lift my handles and follow. When we reach the far edge of the lot and turn around, I lose my grip and the wheelbarrow tips over. I try to quickly bend to the side, wrench upward, but it falls anyway and I have to dance away to keep the weights from sliding onto my toes. I put the wheelbarrow back upright and bend over to pick up the fifty-pound weights, one at a time so I don't slip on the slick snow.

He's watching me so I try to smile. He's grinning wide.

"How could you afford it?" I ask.

"The move? I had some money saved up. I try not to buy anything I can do without, like clothes or a car. I don't have a girlfriend right now either, so that saves me a chunk of change right there."

"How do you make it without a car?"

"I don't need to drive anywhere much. I work from home as a software programmer. I work the hours I want—evenings, week-ends, whatever. So when the gym's open, I'm here. If I need a lift, I just call one of the guys."

"No family around here, though? Or friends?"

He flips his head toward the gym door.

"Just them."

The door opens and Mick steps out.

"Gill says to come in," he says.

Gabe lets down his wheelbarrow and I do the same.

"Just him," Mick says, pointing at Gabe. He walks up and takes his place behind Gabe's wheelbarrow.

"Gotta go," Gabe tells me, and starts to walk away. Then he turns back.

"So I'll see you this afternoon?" he asks. He and Mick catch each other's eye, like they're sharing a joke.

The whole thing's making me feel small, young, embarrassed.

"I'll be here," I say.

Gabe leaves and Mick shoves forward.

"Okay, playtime's over. It's time to turn it up a notch or two," he says.

My arms and shoulders and legs are sore and tight. But I don't say anything—just pick up those handles and push after Mick.

The next day

Everything here is a contest.

Right now it's out of town on the snow-packed road holding twenty-five pound weights to our chests for a mile, then over our heads for a mile, then back home the same. Then again. And again. We've got these rubber things with spikes underneath that fit over our runners, so at least there's some grip, but the cold stings our lungs and burns our eyes, and no one takes it slow. The whole time, we're pushing it to see who gets back quickest.

I can beat Frankie, and most of the time Gabe. Mick's got me, though. Gill leaves us all in the dust. And because I'm supposedly young and fresh, they seem to always manage to make me go a few extra times.

I stop to catch my breath, heaving that icy breath in and out, in and out.

Mick slaps me on the back, pushing me sideways.

"You giving up? We've got three more to go!"

Frankie's got hold of a bunch of old snowshoes he'll bring by next week, so Gill says we'll get a break from the running on the ice and run up hills on the snowshoes instead. While holding those twenty-five pound weights to our chest and over our heads, of course.

Thursday afternoon, 5:20

We're doing the wheelbarrow race again. It's killing me.

Mick stops, points at the door. A couple of twenty-year-olds in tight work jeans stumble out looking like they just got run over by a tank. They went in a half hour ago, looking tough. We know they'll never be back.

The wheelbarrow's tipped over a couple of times already and my shoulders and knees are killing me. I'm a bit jealous of them. Not enough to leave the wheelbarrow on its side and the weights in the snow, though.

Third Tuesday in January, 6:30 in the evening

I know I'll barely make it home tonight, like every night since I started training three weeks ago. It's not just the exercises, it's the sparring too. Throwing punch-kick combinations at Frankie over and over, while he tells me to put more of my hips and upper body into the kicks and more shoulder into the punches, and do it faster every time. Then half the time he grabs a leg and if I'm not careful, takes me down. Getting on my back with Gabe on me and trying to work submissions on him, and when I blow it he pins an arm and hammers his fists down on my face. Good thing I've got the head gear or my face would be swelled up like a pumpkin. Then he slips out from between my legs to side control, laying sideways over my chest. Since he's a fair bit lighter than me, I can throw him off okay, thanks to my wrestling—but not before he's brought an elbow down on my face at least once. And pulled my arm up and behind me into an arm bar, half the time.

When I get home, it'll be tough enough just to stay awake—doing homework's impossible. Part of me wonders if it's worth it. But I know tomorrow I'll pull myself together and show up again.

They don't just save all their brutality for me. They spar with each other every day. Gabe and Mick both have fights coming up in Minneapolis in six weeks, so they're working pretty hard. Frankie and Gill are right in there with them. The four of them go at it like they're out for each other's blood.

You'd never know from the wicked kicks and brutal throws that these guys could still be friends but every time a guy goes down or taps out, the other one helps him back to his feet. When they leave the ring, they're talking about the fight like they were watching someone else, about the mistakes they made and how to be more accurate or agile next time, and which exercises to add to their training to make up for the weaknesses.

The only thing not settled is paying. It still hasn't cost me a dime to train at Top Form. I brought it up to Gill a couple of times but he always walks away to give pointers to one of the other guys.

A half hour later

I'm sitting back on the couch, watching TV, forcing myself to eat the banana and peanut butter sitting on the plate on my lap. I make myself sit up and get the remote off the coffee table, grunting.

I've been watching TV every evening when I get home. Too tired to do anything else.

It's so bad I fell asleep in a test yesterday. When the bell went I still had a page not done. It's the first time I can remember not finishing a test.

Fourth Friday in January, five o'clock in the afternoon

My shins are killing me.

Mick says for muy Thai you have to toughen up the weapons—hands, elbows, legs, feet. So we hit the heavy bags a lot— punch fifty or seventy-fives times in a row to toughen up the hands, kick so that we're making contact with the main part of our shins, over and over, to harden the bones.

I'm doing kicks alongside him, using the new heavy bag Gill got hold of to go with the old one—which, of course, is almost as coated in duct tape as the other one.

Mick's got bones of steel. He can go at it for five minutes straight, one kick after another, a short grunting puff of air out of his mouth every time, until he's drenched with sweat. I'm doing mine half as fast and probably half as hard and still feeling like my shins are mashed. My legs are swollen dark blue. His look like they've never been touched.

He steps back from the bag.

"Had enough?" he asks. It's pretty obvious he could keep going.

I try to look tough. "Only if you have."

He grins and points at the mat. "Take a seat." He sinks to his butt and I sit beside him, trying not to fall as my shins scream at me.

"Don't worry. It gets better," he says after we've sat there quiet for a minute.

"How long did it take you?"

"To get used to it? I can't remember."

I look over at him. "How long have you been doing muy Thai?"

He snorts. "Long enough that I don't remember *not* doing it."

He leans back onto his shoulders.

"We moved to Thailand when I was four. My parents were relief workers. Right away they wanted me and my sisters to learn the culture so we wouldn't be too American. After a couple of months we got a house next door to a muy Thai camp. For the first while my mom kept freaking out because I'd wandered out of the house. She thought someone kidnapped me or I'd got lost somewhere. But after she found me in the camp for the third or fourth time imitating the fighters' moves, they signed me up. That gym was my second home."

"Then when I was fourteen we moved back here to Minneapolis. It was strange—I was white like everyone else and spoke English and everything, but it didn't feel like home. In Thailand I was the skinny white giant. It was obvious I was different from the Thai people around me. Here I looked the same as everyone else, but inside I was Thai. There was one muy Thai gym a half hour from my house so every day after school I'd hop a bus there, and I'd train until dinner, sometimes later."

No wonder the guy's so good.

"Are you a black belt? You gotta be by now."

He sits up. "Muy Thai doesn't have belts. Sometimes different colored armbands or shorts, but not where I trained in Thailand."

"Why not?"

"Muy Thai isn't for the studio. It's fighting, pure and simple. Real-world fighting. You do it, you get hurt. You get bloody and broken in pieces. You know how good you are and how good the other guy is every time you leave that ring. You don't need a belt to prove it."

He stands up and holds a hand down to me.

"Let me show you."

A half hour later

I'm cursing under my breath. Every step hurts. Every cough or deep breath.

I was sparring with Mick a half hour ago and starting to get in some good shots. One of my high kicks caught him in the neck, a good clean shin-shot. I grinned because it was probably the first time in one of our matches that he actually got shook up.

Just like that, he came back at me with a left kick straight to the ribs. I countered with a right hook, put everything I had into it. He ducked and threw another kick in exactly the same spot. I was so surprised I wasn't ready when he charged, shoved me up against the cage, whipped behind and got his arms around my chest. The shot of pain in my ribs sucked the wind out of me and he lifted me up and threw me on my side, hard. I've been thrown a thousand times but never after a guy'd just hacked into my ribs. The pain was so unbelievable that I almost cried.

I jumped up, felt another shot of pain in my ribs and stumbled, half bent-over.

"What the hell was that? You trying to kill me?" I stepped at him, ready to knock him over and pound on his face. He backed up, his eyes wide.

"I told you muy Thai was tough. I was just showing –"

"Shut the hell up! You broke my rib! You think that's cool? You think it's okay? You broke my rib!"

Gill jumped into the ring, put a hand to my rib cage, felt it carefully.

"Breathe in."

It hurt, but not as bad as a half a minute before.

"It could be, but I doubt it. Probably just bruised."

He turned to Mick.

"You better cool it, buddy."

Mick walked up to me, put out his hand toward my shoulder. "Hey, sorry, man. I didn't mean –"

I batted his hand away, gave him a death glare. "Screw off."

That evening

I unlock the door, already thinking about the hot shower that's two minutes away. Push the door open, careful to use just my arms without any body weight.

Crap! At the table, Mom looks up from the sandwich she's holding over a plate.

"What are you doing here?" I ask.

She frowns. "I called in sick."

She's got that look, the one where her eyes are swimming a bit and she's so limp she'll wilt into a puddle any minute.

She looks me over, takes in the light bruises to my face. I straighten the best I can from where I'm favoring the sore ribs and try to fake a smile, but she's eying the spot and frowning.

"You're hurt. What happened?"

"Nothing," I snap. "Just me and some of the guys. You know, you get going, messing around, and one of the guys shoves a little too hard. That's all."

She shakes her head. Her wrinkles are showing now more than ever, especially when she's worked up like she's starting to get now.

"I've seen enough to know that's not true," she says. "Where were you?"

I gulp.

"Out. I told you—with some of the guys."

"I said, where were you?"

I bite my lip.

"Not a good time, Mom. Not right now. Just leave it."

"I will not leave it!" she yells all of a sudden as she jumps up. She's shaking now, like she's going to explode. "You tell me where you were, or God help me, I'll ... just tell me. RIGHT NOW!"

I drop my eyes, walk over, sit down slowly beside her.

"What is it. Your stomach? Did you get in a fight?"

I shake my head. "No, not a fight—well, not exactly. Not a bad one."

"What do you mean by that? What aren't you telling me?"

I look away.

She pulls my chin around so I have to look at her. She seems so beat down, I don't have the heart to turn away again.

"You've been so tired lately, like you used to be after wrestling practice, but it seems worse. You're not training with them again, are you?"

I shake my head. "No."

"Then what? What's got you so run down that you're barely awake every time I see you? You're out of the house before I wake up and then you can hardly talk when I get home after work."

I shake my head. "It's nothing."

"Tell me."

I know from the quiet solid way she says it that she won't let go. I put my hands on the table, lean back in the chair, catch a breath.

"I've been training."

"Training for what?"

I don't say anything but she lets the silence hang there. Stressed or wilted or not, she's going to wait me out.

"A bunch of stuff."

"What kind of stuff?"

I blow out a sigh through my nose. "Boxing. Muy Thai. Grappling. Mixed Martial Arts."

She pushes her chair back, stands up, backs away like I've got AIDS. "What – why – why would you do that?" She paces around the room like a caged animal, shaking her head. "I've heard about that Mixed Martial Arts. People talk about it. It's cage fighting, right? Beating each other without any rules, until one of you is so close to dying that he can't fight anymore? That's what you've been doing? "

I nod my head yes, then shake it no. "It's not like that, exactly."

She points at my ribs. "How?! How is that different from a fight in an alley somewhere? Tell me." She grabs my chin again, pulls it hard toward her even though I resist. "You're going to end up just like your brother, beating people half-dead and getting beat too. Why would you do that? Why?"

All of a sudden, before I know it, I'm slamming my hand flat on the table so loud a cracking sound fills the room and echoes from the kitchen. I catch myself, put both hands flat on the table, try to ignore the pain shooting across my mid-section.

"Think about it, Mom. I'm off the team. I can't wrestle, and I've got nothing else."

"No way. That's not any kind of excuse. You're learning how to beat another man senseless. You can't rationalize that."

I take another deep breath to keep control. My fingers curl around a napkin that's laying there and scrunch it up into a tight wad. I open and close my hands a few times, fighting the urge to yell or leave, or both.

"Don't talk to me about getting beat senseless. I spent my whole life getting the crap beat out of me most days. And you knew it was going on the whole time. You knew Ricky beat me, and you saw the bruises, and you didn't do anything about it."

She hangs her head, then straightens up and tries to look strong.

"It was your father who made you two fight. He said boys had to learn to look out for themselves. I tried to tell him otherwise, but he wouldn't listen. There was nothing I could do to stop it."

I'm starting to boil over again and try to fight it.

"The only thing I learned was how to take a punch," I say as calm as I can. "You wouldn't stand up to Dad. And after he left, you let Ricky keep doing it. You could've called the cops any time, or at least not lied to the school counselor when she asked what was happening to me."

She puts her hands over her face, starts to cry, sinks down into her chair.

"I'm sorry, Ross. You know how I was doing then, what your father did to me when he left with that other woman. You know what it did to me."

"Yeah, I know," I say quietly. I've got hold of myself now, because I see it all clearly, like I saw it all along but wouldn't admit to myself. "I know you didn't have the guts to stand up to Dad or Ricky. You just took everything they threw at you, let them do whatever they wanted. I'm not going to do that. No one's going to run over me again. Not Ricky, not anyone."

I stand up, back away from her toward my room.

"Don't try to tell me I shouldn't learn to fight. Don't say a word. Ever."

I go into my room and shut the door. She's sobbing so I put on my ear buds and turn up the music until I can't hear anything else. Her words go around in my head. "You'll end up just like your brother." I turn the music up even louder until I can't hear myself think anymore.

First Tuesday in February, 9:30 in the evening

It's exhausting just standing here brushing my teeth.

Gabe and Mick are taking it easy now, winding down so they're ready for their fights in a couple of weeks now—bag training and light sparring, some cardio. But that doesn't mean I get off easy. Frankie and Gill are still laying into me and each other like usual. Sometimes it feels like they're going at me harder than each other.

I was too tired to do homework again, too tired to make anything more than a cheese sandwich for supper. It seems like I can barely get through the rest of the day after two hours with Gill barking orders. I'm so sick of stumbling out of Top Form, my body half-broken, just trying to keep my feet lifting high enough that I don't trip. There's got to be an easier way to train.

Two days later

On the way out of math class, Meyers pulls me aside.

"Is everything alright?" she asks. "Anything the school needs to know about?"

The muscles above my knees throb so bad it's murder just

trying to stand straight on the hard floor. But I don't think that's what she's talking about.

"I'm fine," I say.

She studies my face a minute. I look past her at the clock, hoping she'll have to let me go soon so she can get ready for the next class.

"Are you sure? Because it doesn't seem like it."

I take a deep breath, try to smile.

She keeps at it.

"I'm worried about you, because you aren't acting like yourself. You don't seem to be socializing with your peers like you used to. Half the time you're so quiet and withdrawn that you look like the walking dead. I've asked around, and the other teachers have noticed the same thing. Your grades have dropped to the point where you could fail several classes this semester."

I look down, embarrassed. She's right about all of it. I thought I could hide it, that no one would notice. Stupid.

"If there are things going on in your life that you would like help dealing with, there are resources available. That's what Mr. Davies is here for."

I snort. Everyone knows to avoid the guidance counselor. The guy tries so hard he's like the class nerd begging for everyone to like him.

She sighs like she knows what I'm thinking.

"There are others, too. Any time that you like, I'm available, and I know Coach Dahl feels the same way."

I look up.

"Can I go now?"

She sighs again.

"Yes, you can go."

Third Friday in February, 7 o'clock in the morning

I lie in bed a long time, letting myself wake up slowly. There's no hurry, since we're not training today. Everyone but Frankie's in Minneapolis by now, getting ready for Gabe and Mick's fights tomorrow. It sucks not being able to go, but it's a relief to get a couple days off from training.

Spence asked me yesterday if I'd be at the regional finals tournament tomorrow. He seems a bit ticked I haven't gone to any of their meets all year. I told him I'd go. If I can't be at the fight in Minneapolis, may as well. It's better than sitting around at home.

Saturday afternoon, 2 o'clock

It's weird, sitting in the stands. I haven't been in the school gym watching a match from the stands since—well, maybe never. Watching the guys getting ready, running through moves with each other to warm up, pushing each other around a little to blow off steam, checking out the girls in the stands. Spence catches my eye and nods at me, probably glad I took him up on it when he invited me. I nod back.

It feels familiar—the same type of meet I've been in dozens of times in just as many school gyms, ever since I was six. Feels as normal as my own living room. Still, it's hard to believe I was the champion, the all-star, the one who went undefeated all last year. Top Form has sucked in so much of my life that I haven't even thought of high school wrestling most days.

I scan the crowd. There's a lot of kids from Rosslyn, kids I've known all my life. Suddenly, it feels strange to think about that. The same kids, the same school gyms, the same everything, every day for as long as I can remember. Feels so ... small. I think of Mick, growing up in Thailand, learning muy Thai and hanging out with all those kids who were shorter and darker-skinned than him, eating strange food, talking in a strange language. It would be good to go somewhere else for a while.

She's there. Erin. On the next bleacher over. She looks kind of excited, comfortable, like she belongs. She's got on the old Minnesota North Stars hockey jersey that belonged to her grandpa before he died a few years ago. It's still too big on her. Alexis is beside her, laughing.

Alexis looks over, sees me. She doesn't seem as happy now. She gives her head a little shake and turns back to Erin, but she's still not smiling.

The first couple of matches go well. Spence comes out of his with an 8-3 win. He's been working hard, I can tell. His sprawl is way stronger and he's built up the shoulders. Does a nice hip-throw. Then Derek loses his match 5-4, but he works so hard the Rosslyn kids are screaming his name anyway. In my mind it's me down there on the mat working the same moves, feeling the strain and the press of the other guy's strength against mine, executing the take-downs and throwing my weight on his chest, my arm under his shoulder ready to roll him.

But I catch myself imagining the next move—an elbow to his face or knee to the body from side control, maybe an arm bar. All of a sudden the wrestling seems stale, like they're only going halfway. It's still a contest for sure, but there's too many rules. Not the same intensity—too little at stake. You may lose a point or even get pinned, but you're not going to walk away with a swollen eye or a charlie horse so bad you think you'll fall over. Or bruised ribs, I think, touching the spot that's still a bit sore if I twist around too quick.

You won't know how far you could've pushed yourself. Or which of you was the best fighter.

The third match starts. Coach is there, prowling the sidelines, shouting instructions. Just like old times.

I'm ready to leave. Spence is the one I came to see, and he's done. The rest don't matter.

A body squeezes in next to me, shoving me sideways.

"Hey there, tough guy."

I look over and my guts pinch a little.

"Hey, Alexis."

She sits there a minute, letting me squirm. She's always been a bit of a hard-ass.

"What do you want?" I ask finally.

"You're a moron, you know. You've always been a moron. One of these days maybe a light will go on in your head and you'll start thinking for once." She pauses. "Well, probably not."

I didn't come here for this.

"Shut the hell up." I start to stand but she yanks me down.

"You don't get it. You're such an idiot you don't even have a clue."

I yank my jacket out from her fingers, elbowing the guy on the other side of me as she lets go.

"What're you talking about?"

She looks me over, shakes her head.

"You don't even go say hi. She's over there and you just sit here alone like some kind of tortured lonely rebel. It's just pathetic, is what it is."

I'm embarrassed now, not quite getting what she's saying, like my brain's in a fog. Something's not adding up.

"Aw, for – why even bother if you're so blind? You're blowing Erin off, like she doesn't matter. You won't even show she exists. If it was me, I'd tell you to screw off but for whatever reason, you seem to matter to her."

Everything's backwards. She not making any sense. Erin's eight miles above me, way more quality than I'll ever be. I'm a brute she's ... I look past the crowd of heads and bodies, over at her. She's still watching the match, still into it.

"I can't believe you!" Alexis says. "For some reason I don't get, she thinks of you like you're special somehow. But you're treating her like dirt. I mean, you don't talk to anyone lately and that kind of makes sense, since most of those guys are total cave men. But she thought you guys were friends. I guess she was wrong."

She shoves down on my shoulder to push herself up, squeezes down the row back to the aisle and down to the bottom of the bleachers. Her face is tough, a bit mad. She was never the quiet type.

I look across at Erin one more time. She watches Alexis sit back down beside her. They say something to each other before the crowd cheers at something down on the mats and they turn to watch again.

I get up and push my way down the row, hoping Erin doesn't see me as I get down to the gym floor, put on my jacket and head for those big double doors that go out into the hallway. Just like last time I was here.

87

Wednesday morning, 6:30

Gabe's showing me how to sweep from my back when a guy's mounted on top of me on the ground—rotate and then twist and get on top of the other guy. He figured it's the next thing I have to learn because it's how he won his fight in Minneapolis. Just like the guy he beat, I keep taking him down—the wrestling's working huge for me—but almost every time he can sweep me and end up on top. *If* he decides to do that instead of submitting me with one of his jiu jitsu moves.

Mick's sitting on a stool watching. He took a wicked bunch of knees to the body and shots to the head on Saturday, and almost got pounded out before he scrambled to his feet and knocked out his opponent with a high kick to the temple. So he's taking the week off to heal up. In the mean time, he's playing coach, yelling out instructions to me, telling me to use my fists and elbows as soon as I take Gabe down. I may lose to Gabe every time, but at least I'm getting a few good shots in along the way.

"LeClaire! Over here!"

It's Gill, on the other side of the room.

Gabe pulls me to my feet and I step out of the cage.

"What's up?" I yell. He never calls me by my last name.

He just motions me toward him.

I run up and he hands me a couple of kickboxing pads, a little over a foot high and maybe two feet wide.

"I was in the middle of grappling," I say.

He grunts.

"Put them up."

I lift the pads and he throws a couple of high right kicks. I stick out the left pad and the kick jars my shoulder, almost sending me sideways. I steady myself and he takes a couple of quick jabs, a left and a right.

"So you won State last year," he says. I'm surprised, since I never told him anything about it, and almost miss the left knee he throws. The jolt to the pad sends me back a step.

"How'd you know that?"

He throws a right hook and then another left knee, which almost gets through to my body.

"I asked around and some guy at the post office told me all about you. He says you were some kind of local hero."

Is he serious or mocking me? I can never tell. But I catch the words "were a hero." Past tense.

He aims a pair of left kicks and a pair of rights.

"I talked to your coach, Dahl. He seems like a good guy."

I let the pads down.

"What'd you do that for?"

He almost unleashes a high kick, but lets his leg drop and puts his fists to his hips.

"When I've got an under-age kid in my training center throwing his body around like a pro, I have to ask questions. There's no reason I should apologize for it."

He smacks one hand into the other, hard.

"He told me you got kicked off the team for beating the crap out of a guy in a meet. Seems like kind of a dumb move."

He stands there looking at me like I'm supposed to tell him why it wasn't. What's there to say?

"And actually, I wasn't the one who called him," he tells me. "*He* called *me*. He says you're screwing up, that you're close to failing a couple of classes."

"Why'd he talk to you? You've got nothing to do with it. He's not even supposed to know I'm training here."

"Yeah, well, evidently someone told him you were. And actually, I do have something to do with it. A lot, actually. You're gonna have to fix those grades."

He steps forward again quickly, starts doing left-right punches one after the other. I barely whip the pads up in time. My heart's beating fast and my arms are shaking.

"When I started here, you said you weren't my babysitter," I say.

He drops his hands again and steps back.

"Look, kid. I'm new around this town and no one knows me. Anyone who's heard of MMA thinks it's a bunch of gorillas trying to turn each other into road kill, so that's one strike against me already. Pissing off the high school wrestling coach won't help any. If I don't work with Coach Dahl, he could let the word out that I'm making kids into street fighters instead of good upstanding students who finish high school and get good jobs and head off to college. According to him, you're one of those kids who could actually get to college, too, if you keep at it and don't get distracted. By which he means, if I don't ruin your life with MMA."

He points a fist at the door.

"So either you keep your grades up, or you're out."

I'm furious. First, they kick me off the wrestling team. Now he's threatening to kick me out of Top Form. I throw down the pads.

"Screw you."

It's the same cruddy feeling as when I stormed out of the gym after hammering Sorenson. I grab my stuff off the floor, throw on my jacket, and shove the door open. I don't look back.

Two days later

I'm standing in front of the Judo club, next to Sundstrom's Groceries in the strip mall downtown. Last month the Sensei (he likes to call himself that, a kid told me once) renamed it, so the sign that always said "Jong-Qi Judo" now has an extra white banner pasted beside it with the words "and Mixed Martial Arts."

Through the wall-sized window he's leading fifteen kids in pure white uniforms through a bunch of judo moves. The place is outfitted pretty well—new mats, nice punching bags, smooth white walls. A lot nicer than Top Form.

I open the door and step in. The Sensei motions for one of the students to take over the training and walks up to me.

"Good afternoon," he says, taking a half bow. "My name is Sensei Walker. Welcome to Jong Qi Judo Mixed Martial Arts. Are you interested in learning the ways of the warrior?"

For a second I think the guy's joking but he doesn't crack a smile. I put on the most serious face I can work up.

"I'm just curious," I say. "What's your training like?"

He waves his arm in a semi-circle toward the students training.

"We run a disciplined regimen of the most strict and authentic judo. And for those who want to learn the art of more diverse fighting, we offer rigorous training in a variety of martial arts."

He gestures toward the back of the studio. A few kids and a couple of twenty-somethings are punching heavy bags, stopping every thirty seconds to catch their breath and see what the kids around them are doing.

"Excuse me," the Sensei says.

He claps his hands. "Alright, students, that's enough for today."

The group doing the routines breaks up, talking and heading to the corners to pick up their jackets and head out. The guys in the back step back from the bags and start taking off their boxing gloves.

"How long's the class?" I ask.

"One hour, three times a week."

"That doesn't seem like much," I say.

He gives me a look like I'm a child. "Believe me," he says. "After an hour with me, you'll need the day off in between."

I look back at the guys putting away their boxing gloves. Most of them have only faint patches of sweat around their arm pits or down their chests.

"If you are interested," he says, "We run an orientation class for beginners every Tuesday at six o'clock. You should try it out. Don't worry, it won't be too intense to start with."

It takes all I've got not to laugh.

"Yeah, maybe. Say, do you know anything about that other club in town? I think it's called Top Form or something like that."

He waves his hand at the door. "Yes, I've gone by there. From what I saw, it could barely be called a training center. The equipment is sub-par and there were only a few students present. Several people have joined my dojo after trying out Top Form, and found this gym far better for learning the disciplines."

I think about all the guys I've watched walk into Top Form tough and walk out broken, and smile.

I thank him, promise to come by some Tuesday to try it out, and head home.

Second Monday in March, 3:40 in the afternoon

It's freezing cold, waiting for her outside school like this. I whipped out after class to be sure I'd catch her. It's been ten minutes standing here watching kids walk by and feeling like a complete idiot. I can feel the skin on my cheeks freeze up tight. I stamp my feet to try to keep the blood flowing, wishing I owned a good pair of boots, wondering when winter's going to be over.

There she is. Finally. And she's alone, like I hoped.

She sees me from across the street, looks surprised. As she walks up, I bob from foot to foot, nervous, trying to find something for my hands to do besides twitch.

She stops a couple of feet in front of me, like we're squaring off.

"What's up?" she asks.

Aw, jeez. This is going to be tougher than I thought.

"Look, I..."

"You've ditched me ever since Christmas."

I feel like I'm being cornered. This isn't how it was supposed to go.

"Yeah. About that – I'm sorry. It just kind of felt like it was a pity visit when you came over. You know."

"Why would you think that? We've always been friends, right? You don't have to be a jackass just because ... I don't know. I don't know what you were thinking."

This is going way worse than I planned. It would be easy to just run.

"What's going on with you, though, really?" she asks. "Ever since Christmas, you've basically disappeared. You barely talk

93

to anyone, you're never around at lunch, you don't come out to any of the basketball games or wrestling tournaments. You think now that you're not the big wrestling star, you need to hide from everyone?"

I don't know what to say, so I don't say anything.

"If it's still about what you did to that guy during the wrestling match, let it go. I mean, it was pretty bad, okay, and it did kind of screw up the team's chance of taking a title this year. Not to mention getting you booted off for a year."

I clamp my teeth together, kick at the sidewalk. This isn't feeling so friendly right now.

"But you're not a bad guy," she says quickly, like she can tell I'm getting mad. "Everyone knows that. You're the guy who saved that kid Joey Marsden when the guys from shop class had him cornered and said they'd rip off his ears with a pair of tin-snips. They probably wouldn't have done it, but it still took some guts to step in. You've been doing that stuff since you were a kid."

Of course I stepped in, I think. *And not because I'm such a good guy.* Seeing people act like Ricky just pisses me off and it's all I can do to not go ballistic on them.

"And if the teachers didn't like you, they probably would've had you expelled, but they didn't. If it was a different guy who kept falling asleep in class, they'd be furious."

My head jerks up. "They notice that?"

"Duh! It's pretty hard to miss, since you're asleep more than you're awake. Why is that, anyway? You're not getting high, are you?"

"No!"

"Then what?"

Crap. She just said I'm not a bad guy and now I've got to lie. No way am I telling her I'm learning how to kick guys in the head and twist their arms until they quit. Or that I'm doing it so I can beat the living hell out my brother in a few months.

A car drives up. It's her sister Maia. She leans over and pushes open the passenger door, and yells "Get in, girl."

Erin grabs my hand in both of hers.

"Look, I just want to be friends again. But if you won't talk about it, there's nothing I can do."

I just stand there, of course. Like an idiot made of stone. A big stupid statue.

"You don't have anything to say?" she asks.

As usual, I don't. And if I did, I probably wouldn't know how to say it anyway.

She slides into the car and looks back at me.

"I'll see you around, then."

That night

I push back from the desk, rub my eyes. 10:30. There were more assignments to work on than I thought, and the stack isn't that much smaller than it was yesterday. The teachers were pretty good about it, though. They must've talked about it with each other because they're all letting me get caught up with the work I've missed since Christmas.

It's the first time in months that I'm tired from something other than the training. Being away from the gym for two days has shown how draining the workouts really are. Honestly, I don't really miss it right now. Half of me's ready to quit Top

Form, give it a shot at Jong Qi. It might be lame but it'd have to teach me a few moves, at least.

There's one reason to keep at it with Top Form, one solid reason. He's six feet tall, 190 pounds, in automotive school, and coming home soon. When I face him down, every bruise and stiff muscle I go through will be worth it.

I'm doing the math. To keep up, I'll probably have to spend a couple hours a day on homework. Which'll pretty much rule out most of the TV and video gaming. No sitting at the table in the evening, picking at my food for an hour while I try to find the energy to get up. No more falling asleep in class, either, which means getting to bed on time. I'm not sure I can pull it off.

I get up to brush my teeth and call it a night. I'll go by Top Form tomorrow, take another look at it, see if I can train all-out and keep up with school at the same time.

Tuesday afternoon, 3:20

I'm on my way out of school when Coach calls after me. I wait for him.

"LeClaire," he says. "You doing alright?" He looks me over, seems to notice a little bruise that's still under my right eye from sparring with Mick last week.

"Where'd you get that?" he demands.

None of your business, I think.

"I gotta go," I tell him, and step away.

He pulls at me. "You watch out, son. Someday, if you don't straighten out, it'll be too late."

Two hours later

Frankie's pumping weights. Mick, Gabe and Gill aren't around, but a guy I've never seen before is pedaling hard on the stationary bike.

Frankie sits up, calls "Hey, kid!"

He comes over with a bottle of Gatorade, cracks it open and hands it to me. We sit down on the floor.

"You doing okay?" he asks. Jeez. Why's everyone asking that lately, like I've got cancer or something?

"I've been worse."

"Really?"

"Yeah."

He smiles.

"Thought when you stormed out the other day you were gone for good."

"I was definitely thinking about it," I say. "The training's a killer. Wrecks me."

"Yeah, me too."

Frankie lays back. We sit there a minute, watching the new guy cycle like he's going for a world record.

"You know him?" I ask.

He shakes his head. "I've never met the guy. He was here when I arrived, and Gill was on his way out and didn't say anything, so he must be okay."

We watch him a while longer.

"When I was in law school in California, they'd give us stacks of books to read and hammer us with lectures and papers. Then when you thought it couldn't get any worse, they'd throw on these tests that made my brain feel so exhausted I could barely spell my name. I went through it for two years and thought I'd never make it out alive. And that wasn't the worst of it, either, because once you were done, you couldn't just go practice law. First, you had to pass the California Bar."

"What's that?" I ask.

"That," he says, and props himself up on his elbows, "is the mother of all tests. You don't just study for it—you give your life to it, day and night, for months. People spend almost as much time and money getting ready for that test as they did going to school. They hire a tutor and take special classes just to prepare for it. The problem is, I was broke. I couldn't afford the extra help. I was working full-time the whole way through school just to pay the tuition, and still had to get student loans on top of that."

"So what'd you do?"

"I gave up sleeping for a month and a half. I was up at five every morning, including Saturday and Sunday, studied a couple of hours, went to work making work gloves at a leather factory for eight hours, went home and studied til midnight."

"It must've felt good when you passed."

He laughs.

"Yeah, it would've, if I had."

"You didn't make it?"

He puts down his empty Gatorade bottle.

"Sure, I made it. A year later I took the exam again. This time, I quit the job, crashed in my cousin's basement and lived on Raman noodles. I studied 24-7 for two and a half months, and this time I made it. I was lucky, though, because a lot of really bright people take three tries to get it, and some don't ever pass."

"No kidding," I say. "But it felt good when you were done?"

"Best day of my life," he says.

It never occurred to me any of them other than Gabe actually had jobs. Never thought too much about their lives outside the gym at all, actually.

"So you were a lawyer?"

He grins. "Still am. How do you think I can afford this little hobby?"

He gets up and walks back to the weights and picks up a couple of dumb bells.

The new guy's over by the heavy bags, pulling on his gloves. He's big. Six-two, maybe, and way over 200 pounds. He sees me from across the room and nods me over.

"Would you mind holding the bag for me a while?"

He's got a bit of a drawl, like a cowboy out on the range or something.

I shrug and get behind it, put it between my shoulder and head and brace it from behind with both hands. He's got dark brown hair, cauliflower ears, a scar above his left eye. His nose looks like it's been broken a few times at least.

He hits the bag with a series of jabs so fast I can barely keep track, and each one sends the bag hard into me. After a couple of minutes I'm ready to call it quits, but he's barely breathing hard. Then he changes it up. Hook-cross-jab. Hook-jab-cross. Left hook, right hook, left hook. He's jolting my shoulders left and right with every blow and when I leave a bit of a gap between my face and the bag, it whacks against my ear and I have to catch myself so I don't lose my balance. In between I see Gill and Gabe come in carrying a couple of big boxes.

After a few dozen more sledgehammers to the bag the guy drops his hands, steps over to his water bottle, and sets himself onto the ground like an elephant.

I follow him and hold out a hand. "Ross," I say.

He downs half the bottle, wipes his mouth with his arm.

"Travis," he says. "Jackson."

I'm trying to think if I've seen him around town before, but he isn't ringing a bell. He's not the kind of guy you forget.

"Do live here?" I ask.

"Do now. Just came in from Wichita. Kansas." His slow drawl makes him sound either lazy or dumb.

"Why?"

He gets up, grabs a towel off the pile Gill keeps by the wall, and sits back down.

"Outgrew my old camp. Got to where I was doing more teaching than learning. When I heard Gill Sans had started up this place, I gave notice, packed my stuff into the pick-up and here I am."

"You moved here?"

"Sure did."

"For good?"

He looks over at Gill, in the ring trading shots with Frankie.

"Doubt I'll ever outgrow Gill. The guy's a legend."

We sit there a bit, watching Gill. It occurs to me for the first time how much better he is than Frankie. Frankie's pretty solid, but Gill's delivering most of the shots.

Travis turns to me. "Speaking of which, how'd you get in?"

"What do you mean?"

He looks me over. "You're obviously fit and all, but what are you – 17?"

I blush, annoyed at being called a little kid.

"Sixteen."

"And Gill let you into his club?"

"Why wouldn't he?"

Just then Gabe walks by.

"Man, we been trying to push the kid out since day one," he shoots in.

I'm past embarrassed now, moving right on to pissed off. I stand up, half-ready to walk out.

"What are you talking about?" I say.

Gabe laughs. "You mean you still don't get it? We've done everything we could to beat your ass down, ever since the first day you showed up."

He looks at Travis. "The kid gets battered so bad he can barely walk when he leaves the place, but every morning there he is, ready to go at it again. Mick nearly busted one of his ribs, and he still came back."

"The boy's gotta have more to him than that for Gill to keep him around."

Gabe nods and slugs me—hard—in the arm. "He can wrestle. He's got good fighting sense."

I'd feel embarrassed again, but I'm too busy trying to hide how much my arm hurts.

That evening

What the new guy Travis said about Gill has me curious.

I get on the web and do a search on *Gill Sans MMA*. After wading through a couple of entries, I find it. Gill Sans. Gill "The Shark" Sans, they call him. There's a picture—he's there in his thigh-length shorts and puffy half-gloves, crouched in a boxing stance, looking mean straight at the camera. Light brown hair—a little thicker than it is now—tattoo of Chinese words on his chest and a ring of thorns around his bicep. Definitely him.

There's a list of stats underneath. Win/loss record: 33, 6 and 1. Disciplines: mua Thai, BJJ black belt, boxing. Height: 5' 10". Welterweight, 170 pounds.

A few more searches bring me to a bio. Started at twenty-three, with a couple dozen fights in Brazil, Japan and Abu Dabi, before his first shot in the big leagues in the US at 25. Took his first fight by submission in the second round. Won a half-dozen matches after that and was in line for a championship fight when he lost a three-round decision to James "The Silver Bullet" deSilva.

The listings are all from three or four years ago. There's no mention of him since then.

Huh.

I look up the other guys. Except Frankie, they're all mentioned on a bunch of MMA sites, with their nicknames: Mick "The Viking" Thalstrom, Gabe "Four Hands" Hinojosa, Travis "Wrecking Ball" Jackson. They've got pro records. Mick's seven and three, Gabe's four and one, Travis is ten and two.

I sit back, trying to figure out what I'm doing in a gym with these guys.

First Wednesday in April

I'm in this rhythm now. Workout, school, study at lunch, school, study for another hour in Meyers' classroom, train, study in the evening. I make sure to get at least eight hours' sleep, or I won't be able to get out of bed in the morning. I was late for workout a couple of times, but that hasn't happened for a while now.

When I don't have schoolwork in the evening, I'm watching fights and technique demonstrations on the web. Every day of training, every piece of knowledge is getting me one step closer to Ricky. I can *feel* it. I *know* it inside.

The one thing missing is an actual fight. Not just sparring with the guys at Top Form, but out there, with some guy I've never met, someone closer to my own skill level, with hundreds of people watching.

I told Gill I wanted a fight. Yesterday he said he found one—six weeks from now, an amateur event in Spalding, an hour away.

Starting today, my training has a new focus. I'll keep up the fitness training full-tilt for a couple of weeks, but then it'll taper off so I'm at peak energy on fight night. In the mean time, we'll keep on with the skill training and the sparring.

Win or lose, the fight'll show me what I've got. What I can bring against Ricky.

When he shows up in a couple of months, I'll be ready.

Thursday evening, 7:20

I'm pumped, pacing around the apartment.

"Damn! Damn! Yes!"

I submitted Gabe today—an arm bar. Sure, he submitted me two times before that and three times after, and it may have been surprise that got him more than anything—even I couldn't believe it was happening—but I got him once. He tapped.

Friday morning, 6:30

I walk in. Gabe's sitting down on the mat, watching Travis. I join him.

"What's with him?" I ask.

"Looks to me like he's praying."

"What for?"

"What do you mean, what for? To pray. You pray, don't you?"

"....uh...." I'm feeling uncomfortable now.

"Do you?" I ask.

"Hell, yeah," he says. "I mean, *heck* yeah."

I shoot him a look that says "gotcha."

"I'm Catholic. If you're Catholic, you pray. Straight up, simple as that."

He slaps me on the knee as he stands up.

"I just don't pray in the corner in the middle of a workout."

Saturday evening, 9:40

It's him. The moment I catch him in the corner of my eye, I know it. The movie theater's dark, we're into the third trailer already, and he comes around the corner from the half-lit hall—Sorenson, a blonde chick and one of his wrestling buddies, joking and bumping around a bit. Without thinking, I'm jumping halfway to my feet, but I catch myself.

They're coming up the side aisle, between me and the front screen, looking into the dark for a seat. The theater's mostly empty so they pick the row three ahead of me. In the dim light from the main exit I can make out his cocky grin, the one I wiped off his face with my elbow. I look for the bruise or a scar on his nose or cheek but of course it's not there anymore, it's had five months to heal. I heard he got beat bad in his first match at regionals. Which would've been sweet to see, if I'd actually been there winning a match of my own.

They slide their way past a few people toward the middle of the theater, Sorenson and then the girl and then the buddy. They're three rows ahead of me. As they're sitting down, Sorenson's buddy turns and recognizes me. He reaches around the girl, prods Sorenson and points.

"Look, it's LeClaire," I hear him say.

Sorenson squints, catches my eye. Part of me wants to hide. The other part's ready to jump forward three rows and land a fist in his face.

His mouth twists up, mean. He pushes back toward the aisle, bumping the girl. She's looking at me too but when he bumps her, she shoves her hand up to stop him.

"Don't, Matt," she says, hissing like she's angry and irritated. She reaches over and catches onto the jacket of Sorenson's buddy, pulling him back too.

"Just leave it, Jake." She motions at the screen. "It's about to start anyway."

She drags both of them down to their seats. The other guy gives me an evil look before settling in. Sorenson turns around and glares. If he's trying to scare me, it isn't working. I snort and lift my chin at him, pretty much daring him to make some kind of move.

The movie's pretty decent, plenty of explosions and gun play, but I'm distracted. His head is always there, three rows ahead of me. I wonder if he feels my eyes drilling into the back of his skull.

Then the credits are rolling. I'm not sure what to do—get up and leave before they can squeeze down the row after me? My body tenses up rigid at the idea. No way. Somehow, I manage to stay sitting, leaning back, legs up on the empty seat in front of me, like it's no big deal.

Right away Sorenson and the other guy turn around. The girl looks at one of them, then the other.

"Come on, guys, let's just go," she pleads.

Sorenson ignores her. He looks over at his buddy. "Whaddya think—should we?"

"Yeah." His friend gives me a stare that's probably supposed to make me shake.

It's exactly like Ricky and his friend Mac cornering me in the basement, two middle-schoolers picking on a second-grader. The helplessness, them standing over me—it was the worst feeling in my entire life. Knowing something bad's coming, not sure what exactly they're going to do, but there's no way out. Waiting for it was always way worse than actually getting beat on.

I shake off the fear, feel myself getting juiced, ready to take them on. This isn't second grade anymore. I lean forward, put my hands over the seat in front of me.

"If you're hoping I'll run, you're out of luck."

I stand up, start heading toward the aisle. The usher's there, watching us, suspicious. I turn away from him and point at the back exit door.

"I'll meet you out there."

Then I walk past them toward the main exit out the front of the theater to the lobby. I know this is my chance. A couple of quick steps and I can be on my way home, leave them in the back parking lot alone. But I don't. Out the front glass doors to the sidewalk, left around the corner and down the side of the building, and I'm in the back parking lot. There's only a few cars and they're getting ready to head out.

The three of them are just coming out the back exit. When Sorenson sees me he looks surprised and maybe a bit scared for a second, but he gets his cocky grin back right away. Then the girl sees me and grabs onto his arm.

"Don't, Matt. It's not worth it."

But he shakes her off and she dances away from the building ten feet and looks from one of us to the other, biting her nails.

The other guy is out now too. They move apart a bit and take a couple steps toward me. Sorenson's closer.

My first instinct is to step back, size them up, plan my first shot. But I'm not going to be that kid in the corner of the basement waiting to get hit—never again. No way.

I hop forward fast and aim a fist at Sorenson's gut. When he bends down to block it, I circle both hands around the back of his neck and lock them together, pull him down, and throw my right knee straight up into his face, just like Mick taught me. I haven't sparred without headgear since that first day in the ring, so the crunch of my knee into his face is a bit of a shock at first.

He's still standing, so I hop back and let go a looping side kick, lots of hip action, and my shin connects with his temple.

He's on the ground, hardly moving. It's happened so fast his friend hasn't got a handle on it yet.

"Come on!" I say.

The buddy looks down at Sorenson, balls up his fists, faces

me again. The girl's bent over Sorenson now, crying and asking him if he's okay.

The guy takes a step toward me. I jump forward, fake a left and when he goes to block it, nail him with a right hook. His head cracks sideways and before he can recover, I slam my shoulder under his chin, send him stumbling back. He manages to keep his balance, staggers sideways a bit, and crashes against the theater's brick wall. I move closer, ready to tee off on him. He looks up at me, panicked, bends over holding his gut, and waves a hand at me.

"No. No," is all he says.

I'm springing up on my toes now, shoulders pumping. The world's black except for the guy in front of me that I'm about to finish off.

"Come on!" I yell.

He stays stooped down, hand held out in front of him.

"Come on!" I'm screaming now, desperate to feel myself breaking his body, his legs, his head. But he doesn't rise, just stays on his butt against the brick wall, defenseless. I look over at Sorenson and the girl, hear her screaming at me. She's got her hands on his face, his nose is gushing blood on her arms.

Then something snaps inside my brain and I see what I've done.

I turn and run. Through the parking lot, down the dark street between houses, away from the lights of downtown. I slip on some ice, fall onto my shoulder, get up and run some more, as fast I can, breathing so hard the insides of my nostrils burn from the cold.

An hour later

My pulse is pounding so hard my temples throb. I've been pacing around the living room trying to keep from punching the walls. In my mind Sorenson's there on the pavement, barely moving, his girlfriend freaking out, while his buddy hides his head between his knees. Still feel that rush, furious, ready to do worse. It's freaking me out a little. *How far would I have gone?*

When Mom started asking what was wrong, I told her it was nothing, I'd just had too many energy drinks this afternoon. She didn't look convinced.

So now I'm in my room, beating on my pillow, slamming fists into the mattress, cursing as quietly as I can with each blow. It should feel better, beating the crap out of them. Like I won, like I was better than them.

Finally I lean against the wall, calm my breathing. Can't think of what else to do, so I text Erin. She's watching a flick with Alexis at her place, they're just getting into it, but she can pause it. I say not to bother, I'll talk to her tomorrow.

Mom's in her room now so I go back to the living room, turn on the TV and flip channels. The fight's still playing over and over in my mind.

I'm glad Erin wasn't there to see me.

Third Monday in April, 5:30 in the afternoon

I pull the heavy bag off the hook and lay it on the ground to practice my ground-and-pound. The bag is a guy I'm controlling—my chance to inflict major damage.

I straddle it, try to imagine it's a guy, like Gill told me to the first time I did the drill, but it's going nowhere. Gill's already had me doing a lot of bag work today, punches and kicks. I'm tired. The beat-down I gave Sorenson and his buddy is in my head all the time. Them lying there, moaning while the girl screams. The bruised knuckles on my right hand that reminded me about it for two days afterward and are still tender.

I look down at the bag again, try to care. I give it a few blows, but then sit up. I look around the room at the other guys training. It seems like a lot of work just so we can get into a ring for fifteen minutes, if we're lucky enough to last that long.

Every other kid in town is hanging out somewhere, catching a show, chatting it up or texting, eating a burger. I'm sweating and hurting as long as I can take it, just so I can down a protein drink and stumble home and try to get my homework done.

Gill walks up.

"Not into it today, huh?"

I shake my head.

"Well, you can always take off."

I look around. The other guys are all hard at it. The only way they go home early is if they're puking from a stomach bug or too injured to stand.

I shake my head again.

"No thanks."

He looks down at me, skeptical.

"You gotta dig deep and find a reason, or you'll never push through."

I know what he means—the exhaustion, the fear of losing, wondering if I'm wasting my time.

He walks away and I stare down at that bag again. I take a

deep breath and look up at the clock.

I'm punching. Bent over slightly, raised up on my knees but keeping them clamped on the bag, punching and punching. Three minutes. It's Ricky. He's come home and he's bragging and daring me to spar with him again like old times, and I've slammed him to the ground. He's thrashing but he can't stop me, and I'm punching and elbowing. Then two minutes, lying sideways across the bag that is Ricky, keeping him flat while I raise up enough to swing my right knee into his ribs, over and over. Then two more minutes on the other side giving him my left knee. Then back on the bag, three more minutes of punches and elbows.

I sit up, catch my breath, feel the burn in my arms and guts and the insides of my thighs from gripping the bag. He's laying there, bloody, not moving. I've won.

Mick walks by.

"Looks like you killed him," he says, and laughs.

I stare down at that bag. I can't stop imagining. It's not just Ricky lying there. Next to me, Mom and Erin are looking at his broken face and me leaning over him, blood on my knuckles, sweating and heaving in deep breaths. There's horror in their faces, disgust, and Mom has her face in her hands, sobbing. Erin avoids my eyes and just walks away.

I get to my feet, grab my jacket and leave the gym. As I pass Travis, he stops skipping rope, watches me, not saying anything.

Tuesday afternoon, 4:00

First thing when I walk in the door to Top Form, I see Travis. He's yawning, stretching. He motions me over.

"Morning, Squirt. I was talking to Gill and we got something new for you."

He lets his arms drop to his sides and his biceps bulge for a second. The guy's massive—a punching machine. He can take any of us out with a single blow if he gets an opening.

Something about the way he's saying it makes me suspicious. He's trying to act casual but something's going on.

"Fire away."

"It's time to learn the knockout punch. You up for it?"

I shrug. It seems like a reasonable thing to take on, now that I've learned enough jiu jitsu and muy Thai moves and defenses to at least make Mick and Gabe pay attention when we spar.

"You don't look like the knockout type," he says. He cocks his head to the side and gives me the once-over. "Course, you never know. Some people got more behind their fists than a guy'd figure. Let's get you into the cage."

I put on my headgear and follow him, wondering if I'll be coming back out on a stretcher in two minutes.

"If you're gonna get hold of the knockout punch, you gotta be heavy-handed. To get there, you gotta do the weights. You gotta hit the bag." He shadow boxes.

I look at his biceps again.

"No kidding." I've been working the bag every other day since I started at Top Form, and he's seen me do it.

He laughs. "Yeah, but there's more to it. Your arm can only do so much." He swings his fist forward. "Do you see how much force went into that? It didn't have terrible much behind it, did it? Now watch this."

He stands, left foot forward, swivels right at the hips, brings his right hand back with him. Then in slow motion, he twists

112

his upper body back straight and moves his fist out in front of him at the same time. He does it again at half speed. Then again at full speed, his whole body following his hand forward. I can just imagine his opponent lying flat on the mat with a crushed cheekbone.

"See that? The power comes from the hips and from whipping yourself forward. You need that kind of force for ultimate knockout power. Especially if you're at, what, 175?"

I nod. "Yeah, about that."

"So that's how it's done. If you can master that and add the right power drills to it, you're doing good. But there's one other thing."

"What's that?"

"Well, you gotta find the opening, that's what. If you got heavy hands but the guy blocks the punch, it won't do much other than maybe soften him up a little. And if you don't hit him, you open yourself up to a counter-punch. Or worse yet, a kick to the ribs or head. And that, my boy, you do not need."

He points to me. "Okay, now, you try it."

I go through the drill and he does it beside me. Twist at the hips, shoulder as far back around as possible, then a quick snap back, fist slamming forward. I can feel the extra power.

We do that a good twenty times or so, and I'm starting to get confident.

Travis claps me on the back. "That's good, good. Would you want to try it on me?"

I should hesitate, but it'll feel good to use it, help it sink in.

We face off, go through the movements in slow motion, him swinging at me, me doing the twist-release-punch, timed for the opening he leaves when his hands are down, fist to his chin.

Then again, a dozen times over.

"Now faster," he says.

We go up to half-speed, same routine over and over. It's feeling natural. Gradually, he speeds up his punches and I keep up with my knockout punches, faster and faster until we're going all-out. Then he comes at me hard, makes contact, sends me back a step.

"Dodge it," he calls.

We do it again, and he clips me again. Not enough to do damage, but enough to set me back on my heels and want to avoid the next one.

"Gotcha," he says, and grins.

I'm starting to get mad. Like always.

He comes at me again. This time I dodge, twist, slam my fist forward. Right into his face.

He rubs his chin and smiles. "Hey. Nice one!"

I don't say anything back because I'm boiling inside. I lunge, throw a looping right with some twist to it but not full-out. He dodges it and nails me with a hard swift jab that crunches into my cheek bone behind the headgear and jars my head back.

"Careful there," he says, a little less playful this time. "You're leaving yourself open."

I take another big swing, but this time it's all arm, no power behind it and no control. He dodges and slams his fist to my ribs. Probably not full strength, but it knocks the wind out of me good and reminds of when Mick almost busted them on the other side.

I'm not thinking anymore, not doing the exercise. I stalk him and he fades back, circling to my right. I fake a left and when he counters, I twist at the hips only this time I whip my leg out and up. My foot just grazes his head but he's already launching a bomb in my direction. At the last minute he pulls it so it nails my shoulder, but it still feels like I've been hit by a bull. I get up and make one last lunge at him. As I swing, he dances back and to the side and I stumble past him and into the cage, then roll to the floor. I sit up, embarrassed.

He stands over me. "You done now, or you set on getting your ass whipped right into the emergency room?"

I try to calm my breathing down. The bruises to my ribs and shoulder are starting to hurt now. I blew so much energy trying to lay him out, I'm not sure I can even stand up without holding onto the cage for support.

"Yeah. I'm done."

He sits down beside me.

"Listen. You did two things wrong. First off, you blew your wad. Gassed out. You gotta pace yourself. You used up all your energy in what—a minute and a half? In a couple of weeks, you'll have to make it through three three-minute rounds. If you go pro, it's five-minute rounds. In some leagues, they'll even do a ten-minute round to start with and believe me, that ten minutes can feel like a day and a half. Sure, you'll keep training and build up the cardio. Still, there ain't more than a handful of fighters out there who can keep up the kind of pace you just tried, charging around the ring like that. You gotta fight smart—pick your shots carefully, get in and out, then bide your time until the next chance. Does that make sense?"

I take a deep breath.

"Yeah. What's the other thing?"

He pulls me up and we walk out of the cage to the bench and sit down. I pick up my water bottle and drain it in one long guzzle.

"If I ain't mistaken, you were angry out there," he says. "Tee'd off, like it was personal between you and me. But it ain't. You gotta remember that—it ain't personal. Sure, you gotta get yourself pumped up and motivate yourself to pound the guy into the ground. That's the whole point, now, right? But you go farther and convince yourself he deserves a beat-down for his sins, and you lose control. You'll end up pushing too hard and open yourself up every time. And besides, it takes all the fun out of it, because you'll probably go home angry, too."

He starts to stand up.

"I can't help it," I say.

He sits back down.

"What do you mean?"

I can't believe I'm about to say what I'm about to say.

"It's why I came here in the first place."

"Let me guess," he says. "Your dad?"

"Kind of..."

"Okay, I'll go down the list. Step-dad?"

I shake my head.

"Brother?"

I don't respond.

"Bingo!" he says.

The guy's pissing me off for getting it right. Ricky's been my secret. I never told anyone outside the family what he did to me, although people probably guessed. And I sure never told anyone I was training so I could pay him back for every single shot and kick and whipping he ever gave me. It's my secret. At least, I thought it was.

"How'd you know?"

He shrugs. "Talk to these guys, or to guys in any MMA gym

116

in any city. A good half of them or more get into the cage for the same reason. You grow up angry and you learn how to fight. Most of all, you learn how to take a shot and handle the pain. Am I right?"

I nod.

He looks away, like he's thinking hard about something.

"What you have to remember is, there's nothing wrong with being angry. It's what you do with it."

He points to the ring, where Mick is busy shadow-kick boxing.

"Looks like I have to go teach Mick how to lose without getting angry," he says, grinning.

He gets to his feet.

I stay down, try to relax, to imagine fighting without Ricky in my head. I don't think I can.

Last Friday in April, five o'clock in the afternoon

Gill's gone today. Mick, Frankie, Travis and Gabe are all here, like usual, working out.

I walk into the middle of the room so they're all close by.

"Guys," I say.

A couple of them grunt hello, but they don't stop what they're doing.

"Guys! Stop, okay?"

They finish their reps and look at me.

"What's up, sprout?" Travis asks.

"You know the first couple of days, when you did your best to bash me out of the gym?"

Gabe and Mick chuckle.

"What about it, buddy?" Frankie asks.

"I want you to do it again."

They just stand there, looking confused.

"What do you mean?" Gabe asks.

"I want you to take it to me. Give it all you got. Take me down. Three minutes each."

Gabe shakes his head. "Why would you want that?"

They're all looking at me hard, waiting.

"My fight's three weeks out. It's making me nervous. I gotta know what I can do, how much damage I can handle. Find out my limits." What I don't tell them is the nightmares I've been having about Ricky beating me half dead, worse than all the other beatings he gave me before, beat so bad I can't get up, and then he stands over me and brings his foot down on my face. It's the same every time. I need to kill the dream. If I can take on all four of them one after the other and walk out of it alive, I'll have proven to myself I can make it past Ricky.

"No way," Frankie says. "We didn't even give you half a beating last time, and you had a half a week break in between. You can't do the shark tank with all four of us giving you our best. You'll never make it."

I stand tall, hands on my hips. "And I think I can."

The others don't say anything.

"Come on, guys. I've been working out with you twice a day for four months and bring it all every time, just like you do. You owe me this."

They look at each other. Mick shrugs, twists his mouth up and raises his eyebrows.

"He's got a point there."

They give a collective shrug.

"Who's first?" Gabe asks.

"You choose," I say, and head into the ring.

Two hours later

The face in the mirror barely looks like me. Puffed-up face, cut over one eye, bruises on my arms, welts on my ribs and legs. If my nose isn't broken I'll be amazed. It's hard to imagine how bad it'd be if I wasn't wearing the headgear.

It was hell on earth. Not at first, though. Mick threw everything at me but I kept my cool, avoided as much as I could, got in some heavy shots and a few good elbows and knees. But he wore my leg down with a half-dozen kicks to the left thigh, and at the end of his three minutes I was having a hard time putting weight on it. Then Gabe came in and took it to me. I shot for a take-down five times but with the damaged leg I couldn't do it quick enough. He backpedaled and I stumbled after him, earning a couple of knees in the head and a nice right uppercut to the chin. When I finally got him down, he swept me, got on top, and reigned down blows on my face. I managed to buck him off and roll so I was on top, and hit him with some good fist and elbows, but he submitted me with an arm bar that I let him hold a little too long, so my elbow's strained.

I massage it now with my other hand a bit. I hope it'll heal.

Then Frankie stepped into the cage and gave me pretty much the same treatment as Mick and Gabe—punches, kicks, taking me to the ground, clinching against the cage to wear me down. I lost my cool by then and charged him, throwing hooks, aiming for the knockout but without any of the form Travis taught me. Frankie took advantage, countering with jab after jab until I was so stunned I had to lay off. But I caught my breath and with a few seconds left, Frankie aimed a looping right at me. I dodged right, twisted my hips and sprang back with a heavy right, using the right form for the first time in the round. My fist made contact and he fell back, almost lost his balance. That earned some hoots from the sidelines.

Through the whole match, the guys who weren't fighting were in my corner giving advice. Some of it I listened to but in the heat of the fight, I mostly did my own thing, and paid for it in the end.

Then Travis closed it off. I figured he'd want to stand up, beat me with his heavy hands. So I shot at him, took him down a few times. He muscled his way back up right away every time, though, and either tossed me away or gave me a shot to the face. By the fourth or fifth time, I finally got some sense—faked a shoot, and when he went down to defend, let go a kick with a good amount of snap to it and clipped him in the head, making the most satisfying smacking sound. I think he was more surprised than stunned, but he staggered back and I rushed him, swinging. Then in one quick move I should've seen coming, he grabbed me round my legs just below my waste, picked me up, carried me to the cage, and slammed me down, all two hundred and some pounds onto my chest. I laid there dazed and tried to squirm out but the guy was just too big, and he kept himself close so there was no room to sweep or even try a submission. He wound up for a shot to my head but just then Frankie rang the bell and the round ended, which was a good thing or I might not've made it out of the cage alive.

It occurs to me now what a coincidence it was, the bell going off right then. One good shot from Travis and I'd have had some serious damage. Seems like maybe Frankie was making sure I made it out alive. I'll have to thank him on Monday.

As I stumbled out of the cage, they sponged my cut and clapped my back and asked if I was alright, and poured water in my mouth and over my head. After walking around a minute, I fell back onto a bench. That's when the pain started. Every part of me hurt, even my hands and the bottoms of my feet. Like I said, hell on earth.

But that's why I did it on a Friday afternoon. I knew it'd be bad. Now there are two days to recover before school Monday morning.

I grab a couple more Ibuprofen from the cabinet and limp to the kitchen for a glass of water. Three protein shakes and a half gallon of Gatorade are already in my belly. A little too much, maybe, but my body was screaming for help, for the energy to stand.

The sound of a key scraping into the front door lock. The clunk of the lock opening, and Mom's coming in the door.

She takes one look at me and drops the plastic grocery bag.

"Ross! O my gosh. Are you okay?!"

She rushes to me and puts a hand on my cheek. I pull back, wincing.

"Jeez, Mom."

She stands there, looking me over, shaking like she's having a seizure.

"What ... what happened, Ross? Who did this to you?"

121

"No one, Mom."

She chews on her lip, glares at me.

"Don't tell me no one did this to you! You didn't fall down the stairs. Tell me, dammit! Who did this?"

I push past her, sink onto the couch. She follows me.

"I asked them to."

"You what? Who? Why would you ask someone to beat you to within an inch of your life?"

"The guys at the gym. I've got to toughen up so..." I stop short of telling her about the fight.

She puts her hands to her hips. She's gone from concerned to angry in two seconds flat.

"You big dumb kid! How can you be so stupid? You got yourself broken up and bruised, just so you can be ready for someone else to do the same thing? That's stupid beyond words! And what kind of adults would do this to a sixteen-year-old?"

"Oh, for – it'll heal up. It's just bruises and a couple of cuts. Bruises and cuts heal. Ricky proved that often enough, didn't he?"

That one catches her, takes her breath. She sinks down onto the chair, puts her head on her hands.

It's a hundred percent obvious what's going to happen. She'll sit there dazed and crying half the night before she passes out, some time around three in the morning. I'll have to look at a half-dead gray-haired beat-down forty-five-year-old woman for the next two days until she finally comes back to life again.

I stand, try to keep my beat-up left leg from giving out.

"Jeez, mom. Get a grip."

Saturday afternoon, 2:20

I groan, walk to the kitchen, put the little frozen pizza in the microwave.

I've applied ice to my cheek, my shoulders, my neck, my legs. By nine this morning I ran out of ice, so I used the bag of peas we had in the freezer, and then the bag of hash browns. After that I resorted to the last thing left, a frozen pizza. The thing thawed in a few minutes. I figured if it wouldn't help with the swelling, it might as well be lunch.

So I'm out of ice, out of pain killers. Worst of all, out of food. No meat, no protein powder. Nothing to rebuild the muscle. Mom's still in bed—she only came out to shuffle to the bathroom and then back to bed. I doubt she'll be heading out any time soon.

I go to the bathroom and check myself out in the mirror. I thought this morning maybe the bruises would've gone down a little. If anything, they look worse than last night.

The microwave beeps and I grab the pizza, scarf it down in three bites. My stomach growls. I'll have to go out.

I grab my Rosslyn Lions wrestling hoodie, pull it on slowly, trying not to cry out like a baby. I look around for mom's purse, find it in the corner behind the table, take out all fifty-two bucks and stuff them in my pocket. Then I pull on my running shoes, trying not to cry again.

Sunglasses. Need to hide as much of my battered face as possible. I find them under a pile of newspapers on the coffee table. In a rare fit of responsibility, I grab an old envelope from the utility bill and write a note on the back telling Mom I took all her cash.

An hour later

The cart's got as close to fifty-two bucks' worth of food as I could figure. I started with the box of burritos and a case of protein shakes, then a jar of peanut butter, and worked my way down from there. It took a lot of aisle-wandering to find the best stuff I could afford, which meant a lot of trying to avoid other people. Every touch to my body hurts.

I've spent so much time trying to hide how broken my face is that it's taken a lot of time to actually find the cheapest of each food item. The hoodie and sunglasses must help, but anyone close up is sure to notice. So far no one's recognized me, although I had to turn around quick and rush to the next aisle to avoid Spence's mom.

I head for the checkout stand, scanning for people I know. It's all clear. My eye catches a display of salt and vinegar kettle chips at the end of the aisle twenty feet over. The salt and calories—I gotta have it. The thing is to figure out what to take out of the cart to make up for it. Tempting as it is to dump the broccoli, it's got to stay. Same with the carrots. The bag of iceberg lettuce—that can go. It was mostly for mom, anyway, and it'll probably be another day before she eats anything but oatmeal anyway.

I'm halfway to the chip display when I know it was a huge mistake.

Coming around the corner from the vegetable section—it's Erin's mom. She sees me and waves.

"Hi there, Ross!"

For a second I think of bolting, but there's no hiding now. I wait for her to come close.

"How are you –" she gasps, comes to a stop. Guess she saw the bruises and swelling. Crap.

Now it's even worse. Erin's coming up behind her.

The three of us stand there, frozen—them horrified, me embarrassed.

Erin breaks the silence. "Oh my God, Ross. What happened? Did you get in a fight? Did someone jump you? What?"

There's no way out of it. If I just leave, they'll call or come over and maybe report it to the school in case it's abuse at home, which'll only make it worse. I knew Erin would have to find out about my training eventually, but meeting her and her mom in the supermarket with a face that looks like raw hamburger is probably the worst way it could happen. It's like a replay of last night, with mom. Only I actually care what Erin thinks.

"I – "

What's the best way to say it?

"It's not what it looks like."

"What is it then, exactly?" her mom asks, concern all over her face.

"It's from ... I was training. For ... well, I've been going to an MMA gym."

Her mom looks confused.

"MMA—what's that?"

"Mixed Martial Arts, mom," Erin says. "It's where guys learn how to beat each other up in a ring. The winner is whichever one makes it out alive."

I decide not to point out it's in a cage, not a ring.

"That's not fair!" I say. "No one dies. Almost no one ever gets hurt that bad, even."

Her mom looks me over, studies my face, raises her eyebrow. "Really."

I touch the bruise on my cheek.

"Yeah, well, I asked them to do this."

"You what? Why would you do that?"

"It's part of the −"

"Do you feel like it makes you more of a man? Is that it?" Erin interrupts.

I think back to when she said wrestling makes guys aggressive and know exactly what she's thinking now. Next to MMA, wrestling looks like preschool gym class.

"Do you really enjoy a sport where guys beat on each other until they're bloody and broken and knocked out? That's not you, Ross. You're better than that."

She reaches for my face. I pull back.

"There you go. Now you know the truth. Yeah, that's me. I like to fight, and I like to train to fight. If that's not good enough for you, I guess that's too bad because it's who I am. Okay?!"

Erin's face goes pale.

"I'm sorry. I just −"

I turn to her mom.

"Sorry you had to see me like, Mrs. Magnuson. Really, I am. But it's not that bad. Everything'll heal up in a few days. So you don't have to tell anyone about it. It'll all be okay soon enough."

Erin steps toward me.

"Ross, I −"

"Forget it." I turn away, leave the cart and walk out.

It Looks like dinner will have to come from the gas station convenience store.

Monday morning, 6:45

Don't ask me why I'm here in the gym. Most of me still aches like I walked away from a car wreck.

Mick looks up.

"Holy crap!" he shouts. "What're you doing here? Go home and rest!"

Frankie and Travis shake their heads like they can't believe it either, like I'm just a dumb kid. Which maybe I am.

Then Gill comes out of the bathroom, stops short. There's a look of horror on his face that quickly turns to anger.

"What the hell happened to you?"

I don't say anything.

He turns to the other guys.

"Do any of you know?"

No one says anything. Gabe studies his feet. Mick looks like he's trying to fade into the wall.

"He asked for it," Travis says. "He wanted into the shark tank. He practically begged."

"And you listened to him? A stupid sixteen-year-old tells you to beat the crap out of him, and you listen? Do you know what kind of trouble I can get in? They could shut down this gym. You guys want to get arrested?"

He looks me over again, shakes his head.

"Damn," he says quietly.

I don't move. No one moves. No one makes a sound.

"You can't go to school," he says. "Does your mom know about this?"

I nod. "Yeah."

"Is she pissed?"

"Yeah."

"Do you think she'll report us?"

I shake my head. She barely got out of bed yesterday and it's eighty percent sure she'll miss work herself today.

"Call her. See if she'll call the school and tell them you're sick. Then these morons can get you some ice packs and heat pads and try to nurse you back to normal."

He looks around at all the guys, shakes his head again like we're a bunch of idiots, and stalks out the front door, slamming it after him.

It's quiet for a few seconds, everyone avoiding each other's eyes.

"Well, that went well," Mick says, and Gabe gives a quiet chuckle.

Thursday afternoon, 1:30

I'm slipping my science textbook back in my locker when a hand clamps on my shoulder.

"LeClaire."

I turn. Coach claps me on the back.

"I've been keeping my eye on you," he growls.

What does he mean by that? I replay the five minutes in front of the mirror this morning. I could swear my face was healed up enough that no one would notice. Does he know about the fight with Sorenson outside the theater? What?

He smiles.

"Don't look so shell-shocked," he says. "You must know I spoke with that MMA trainer, Gill, a while back. Are you still training with him?"

I nod.

"Well, I think it's barbaric, this cage fighting stuff. He seems like a good enough guy, though."

What's he getting at? Is he here to try to get me to quit Top Form? Cause it's way too late for that.

"I checked with your teachers about your grades. It sounds like you're holding your own."

I breathe a little easier.

"Thanks."

"In fact, they say your grades have actually improved over last semester and the year before, and you're hardly falling asleep in class anymore. That's very impressive stuff, kid."

I'm trying not to care what he says but I blush anyway.

"Are you thinking about next year yet?" he asks. "The season's over now so your suspension is, too. We're ready to start training in the next few weeks."

This one takes me by surprise. Wrestling wasn't anywhere in my universe lately.

"I – I don't know. I mean ..."

"You're coming back," he says, like it's a fact. "You're too good not to. You owe it to yourself."

Something happens in me. It's like he's flipped a switch and a wall's sprung up between us all of a sudden. He worked with me for ten years straight and he wasn't exactly a father, but sometimes it felt close. He kept me in line, forced me to work and get better and never stop getting better. But it's not like that now.

"I don't know about that. I might come back, but maybe not. I'll see in a couple of weeks."

He looks surprised, suddenly upset.

"What do you mean? You can't honestly give up wrestling for that fight stuff."

A couple of freshmen walk by just then and turn, surprised by Coach almost yelling.

He lowers his voice. "Don't do it, Ross. An angry kid like you doesn't need to do something that makes him even more angry. It's no good for you."

I think about the guys in the gym. They beat the living crap out of me on a daily basis, but no one's ever treated me bad. Never made fun of my lack of skill. They push me just like they push themselves. The beat-down I gave to Sorenson and his buddy has played through my mind a hundred times since, and it doesn't feel good any of the time. It's the only thing I'm ashamed of from the first day I stepped into Top Form.

"Huh. That's funny," I say. "It doesn't feel like I'm getting any worse."

His face is turning red now. He's looking around the hall, like he's hoping someone will come help convince me. "Don't fool yourself, son," he says. His voice is getting louder, he's talking quicker.

"Don't judge what you don't know," I shoot back. It surprises me, telling him off like I'm his equal. "You said yourself, I've held up my end. I've worked my ass off, shown up here every day ready to give it a hundred percent, kept my nose clean. I'm more in control than I ever was before."

The bell rings.

"I gotta get to class. Wouldn't want to let my teachers down."

I push past him, not looking him in the eye.

Saturday, dinner time

The doorbell rings as I take a mouthful of pork chop.
Mom gets up to open it.

I gag, almost puke up the meat.

It's Ricky. He struts in carrying the duffel bag that holds
everything he owns, and throws it across the room so it skids
across the coffee table, knocking off all the magazines and the
dirty plate I was supposed to clean up, and lands on the couch.
He shrugs off his jacket and lets it drop to the floor.

He's a little skinnier than last time I saw him, and his black hair
is cut short, which I remember now the automotive school made
him do so it wouldn't get caught in a car motor or something.

"Ricky!" Mom says. She's surprised but not totally excited.
It's hard to tell if he notices. Or cares.

"Surprise! I'm home early!" he says, as if it wasn't obvious,
and gives her a half hug. Then he pushes away from her, walks up
to the table and grabs the meat off my plate with his bare hand.

"Hey, fairy-boy," he says, and rips off a mouthful of pork.

I don't do anything to stop him. I'm too surprised—plus,
I'm stuck in the chair. My whole body screams to jump up, but
he's standing right over me. Grabbing at him would only make
him laugh. I stare down at the table, trace the scars that run
across it from years of eating and homework and the toy cars
and trucks I drove across it when I was little.

Ricky takes a big swallow, reaches over me and grabs my
glass of milk. A bunch spills on my shoulder as he pulls it up.

"Ooops, sorry, buddy." He gives a little laugh and bumps his
elbow into the back of my head. "Won't happen again, I swear."

I'm swinging around to my left, my elbow high above the

back of the chair, straight into his gut, and I spring up, slamming my right forearm into his neck. His head buckles forward as the momentum pushes him backwards, me following.

He back-pedals into the coffee table and it cuts his legs out from underneath him and he falls backward onto it with a crash that cracks it down the middle. I almost jump on him but stop short.

I hop back a step, bouncing on my feet, fists up.

Mom's hiding in the corner behind the table, holding herself across the stomach, her face twisted up like she's sick and scared at the same time.

"Come on! Get up, bastard!" I hear my screams like they're coming from outside me, from someone else.

Ricky's got the look of a cornered pit bull—all hate and anger and bits of spit flying out of his mouth.

"You – are – so – dead!" He scrambles out of the wrecked bits of particle-board coffee table. A line of blood seeps from a cut on his arm.

I'm playing out the fight in my mind, like I'm getting ready to spar. What to do if he swings at me. If he lunges. If he kicks. When to block, duck, step out of the way. When to attack and counter. It's all there. And I know his moves—I've seen them a million times, felt what they can do.

But he hasn't seen mine. All he's seen his whole life was me trying to block his kicks or huddling under his punches or charging at him, swinging wild, any time there was an opening.

He rushes me, just like I expect.

It's wrestling 101. I duck under him, using his momentum to push up, twist and flip him over to his back. Immediately I'm on him, straddling, and bring down a heavy right to his face. He doesn't know what hit him. My left fist is coming down now but I pull it back so it just grazes his cheek.

I jump backwards, up and away from him, fists up again.

His face is more twisted with hate than I've ever seen it.

He screams something unintelligible, jumps up, steps at me, and throws a right leg at my head. It's his signature move, the one he's laid on me a hundred times before—and I've run it through in my mind dozens of times. I stick out my left arm to block it, and his foot still makes contact, but even as he starts smiling my hips are snapping forward and my fist slams into his lips and nose.

He falls backward. I stand there at the mouth of the hallway, bouncing on the balls of my feet. I figure he'll try one more time at least.

He jumps up swinging, uncontrolled, each shot meant to knock me out, but I duck, bob right, and crack his ear with my left elbow. He staggers, slams into the hallway wall, but turns back quickly. His ear's bleeding.

Now it's my turn. I wait until he steps forward a bit, fake a shot like I'm going to take him down. Then when he bends down to stop me, I straighten, plant my left leg, and let fly with a right leg kick that has every bit of snap I can give it. It's loose, solid as it flies at his head. My shin hits his temple and slams him to the left like a bobble-head doll. He spins down onto what's left of the coffee table and lies there, stunned, blinking. For a second I wonder if he can see. But he shakes his head, puts a hand to his temple, and glares up at me. He's hurt, sure, but he and I both know it's more about him being helpless. It's me, little Rossy, the kid who gets beat on, standing over him, ready to take him down again any second.

I nod at the door.

"Go."

He doesn't move.

I flick my foot at him.

"It'll only get worse from here."

He gives me one more glare, puts his hand up to where blood's trickling from his forehead down beside his left eye. Then without a word he rolls over to his feet, brushes bits of coffee table remnants off his body, scoops up his jacket. He glares at me one more time. Then at Mom, who's still huddled in the corner, crying. Then he throws the door open and stalks out, pulling it closed behind him with a force that shakes the windows.

It's deathly quiet now. Me, in the middle of the room. Mom in the corner. The coffee table strewn across the floor, along with the upset dining chair.

I walk over to Mom, lower down beside her, put my arm around her shoulder and pull her head to my chest. Her body's heaving, so I hold her close, pull tighter so she can't move.

We sit there like that, neither one talking. I look down at her gray curls and try to believe this broken middle-aged woman was ever young and pretty and happy. Slowly, her body settles and her breathing slows to normal.

"He's gone, isn't he."

I know what she means. Gone forever.

"I think so," I say back quietly.

She takes a deep breath and pushes up. I stand with her and pull away.

She brushes the hair from her face.

"There's another pork chop in the frying pan," she says, and steps toward the kitchen.

Suddenly the door crashes open. It's Ricky, looking crazier than before, his whole face a shaking, trembling firebomb ready to explode. He's got a tire iron in his hands and his eyes are aimed dead straight at me.

"Now, let's go!" he screams.

He steps at me and I jump back, looking around for something to defend myself with, trying not to panic. But there's nothing. I wonder in the back of my mind what the cops'll find when they show up. Whether I'll be breathing or not.

I stand there, hands out, ready to deflect the blow the best I can, maybe find a way to jump in and take a shot at him.

"Stop it!"

Mom's screaming now, all of a sudden standing between Ricky and me, facing him with the cast iron frying pan in her hand, raised up like she's going to hit him.

"Stop it!" she screams again. "Do you hear me? Stop! He's your little brother!"

He's still got the tire iron raised above his shoulder and he's looking past her right at me, his face wrenching against itself in fury. But he doesn't move.

None of us move. We're just standing here, frozen, our chests heaving as we suck in air.

Slowly, Ricky lowers the tire iron so it dangles at his side. He looks at me like I should tell him what's going on. Only, I don't know that myself.

"You were supposed to love him," Mom says, still angry but not screaming anymore. "It was your job to watch over him. You were supposed to stand up for him, not knock him down. But you abused him. You abused him, and your father encouraged you, and I let you. I let you."

She starts crying again but wipes the tears away angrily.

"Well I'm not going to let you hurt him anymore. No more, Ricky. Do you hear me? Do you hear me?"

She just stands there a minute, catching her breath, looking him in the eye. Then she lowers the frying pan, lets it drop to the floor.

"You're lucky. You know that, don't you? Ross could have done back to you all those things you did to him over the years. If he wanted to, he could have beat you until you couldn't walk any more. He could have easily sent you to the hospital, but he didn't. He let you walk out of here with only a few bruises when he could have made you pay for everything you did."

Her face shifts from furious to concerned to just sad. She reaches out a hand, but he flinches away. She lets it hang there, straight out, for a few seconds before it drops. It looks like she's ready to run at him, hug him maybe.

She's crying again. No sniffling, just a few tears rolling out from the corners of her eyes, down past her jawbone.

"Ricky," she says, "you are my son, and I love you, and I've always loved you. But you have a lot of things you need to fix. A lot of things."

Ricky looks like he's in shock, like he's barely hearing her. She puts her hand on his cheek, and he startles like she woke him up.

"I'm sorry, Ricky. I can't believe I'm saying this, but you need to leave now. You need to go far away. Maybe you can come back someday. *Maybe*. First you've got to fix what's wrong in there," she says, and taps a finger at his heart. "Do you understand that? Son?"

He nods—not much, just a twitch of his head, but a nod.

"Maybe you'll be ready to be part of this family again. I hope so. But it'll take a lot of work, and a lot of time."

He nods again, a little more this time. His face is blank. He's not looking at Mom or me. His hand opens and the tire iron bangs onto the carpet.

He's just standing there, and Mom seems like she's said everything she's going to. So I reach over to the couch and throw the duffel bag and it lands at his feet. Without a word, he picks it up and turns toward the door.

"Do you need anything? A sandwich?" Mom asks.

It's a lame thing to ask and I think she knows it, but she still looks for an answer. He shakes his head without turning around, opens the door, and he's gone.

The door thumps closed. Mom and I just stand there looking at each other. I think we're both wondering who that woman was who just stood up to Ricky.

She smiles. "It was a little late, but I did it, didn't I?"

"Yeah, you did, Mom."

She points at the bits of coffee table strewn across the carpet. "Pick that all up and throw it out on the patio, would you?"

I nod.

When I'm done, she comes back from the kitchen with two mugs in her hands. We don't say anything—just sit down there, on the couch, sipping our hot chocolate. I pick up the remote and turn on the TV.

After a minute she reaches over and pushes the off button. She leans back and looks at me.

"I should've done that a long time ago. I'm sorry."

"It's okay," I say back. And we take another sip.

137

The next morning

My alarm's beeping. 5:30. I should get out of bed.

I smell bacon.

I look at the time. 8:30.

Crap! I pull on the jeans and shirt I was wearing last night and stagger into the kitchen.

"I'm late!"

Mom's in her housecoat by the stove, flipping a pancake. She points to a plate full of them and another piled high with bacon.

"Good morning, sweetheart. I made breakfast."

I can't remember the last time she called me sweetheart. Or made pancakes. Definitely not since Dad left. It's a good day if she's out of bed by ten, huddled over a bowl of cereal.

"Why didn't you get me up?"

She smiles, gives me a half-hug over my shoulder.

"Relax. You've earned a little break," she says.

That one comes out of nowhere, almost bowls me over.

"Earned? What do you mean?"

She flips the last pancake out of the pan, picks up the plates of bacon and pancakes and walks past me to set them on the table. She gestures to one of the places she's set and I sit down in front of it. She sits at the other and pushes a bottle of syrup over to me.

"I saw what you did last night."

Of course you did. You were right there, I think.

"It occurred to me afterward—is that why you've been training at that fight club? So you could beat up your brother when he came back?"

I nod slowly. "Mostly."

She laughs. "Well, you got pretty damn good at it. The way

you handled yourself last night sure surprised me, and I know it surprised your brother. You worked harder at that than anyone in this family has ever worked at anything."

I can only mumble a "Thanks" and stick a fork-full of pancake in my mouth.

She puts her hand on mine.

"The thing I'm proudest of, though, is how you handled Ricky. If you'd wanted, he'd be in the hospital right now, or worse. God knows, he earned it a thousand times over. But you held yourself back. I know you did the least damage to him that was necessary to get him out of this apartment. He's very lucky to have a brother like you."

She dishes a couple of pancakes onto her plate and gets ready to eat.

Seems like as good a time as any, I think.

"So Mom ..."

"Yes?"

"There's a fight coming up next week."

"What do you mean, a fight?"

I swallow hard.

"An MMA fight. I'm entered."

She looks away, studies the wall.

"A fight. Are these kids or adults?"

"I don't know. But they'll be my own weight class."

She's still not looking at me.

"Do you wear some kind of protective gear?"

"A mouthguard and cup, and padded gloves."

"But no headgear?"

"Nope."

"And they kick and punch, like you did to Ricky last night?"

139

I gulp. "Yeah."

She's quiet. All I hear is the old clock we got when grandma died, ticking away.

"They have rules, don't they, like no stomping each other on the head and no breaking each others' arms? That kind of thing?"

"Yeah. No one usually gets hurt. Other than a lot of bruises and maybe cuts, of course."

"Of course," she mumbles.

Finally she turns to me with a half-smile.

"Then you better give it a hundred per cent. I don't want to be visiting my little boy in the hospital again."

Wednesday evening, 7:15 – three days before the fight

Gill's across the table from me, pouring cream into the coffee the waitress set down in front of him a minute ago. It's the first time he's ever taken me out. There's got to be a reason.

"So what's up?" I ask.

He opens a sugar packet, dumps it in the cup, stirs it, takes a sip.

"You need to prepare yourself for the fight. Mentally. In that ring, in front of people, it's a whole different thing."

"Like how?" I ask.

He settles back in his seat, lays his hands on the table with the cup halfway between them.

"At the start of the fight, the first thing that's gonna happen is the adrenalin dump. You'll get pumped up and explode with everything you've got, and he'll do the same. But if one of you doesn't knock the other guy out or get him to the ground right away, you'll have to keep fighting. And now that you've spent that adrenalin, you'll feel wiped out. Your arms'll be heavy, your legs'll drag, you'll be short of breath. Your only hope is that the other guy feels the same way.

"The other thing could happen is you doubt yourself. Maybe the guy's got the look like a pit-bull in his eyes. Maybe he's got tats of daggers and vipers over half his body. Maybe he's ripped like Arnold. What you gotta remember is, the bigger guy doesn't always win. The meaner guy isn't necessarily any more fit or skilled or prepared than you are. Even if he is, anything can happen in the cage. You just have to find his weak spot before he gets to yours."

He takes a sip of coffee, looks me in the eye.

"The other thing to remember, the hardest thing, is at this point it doesn't matter whether you win or lose. You're an amateur. This is your first fight, you're just getting your feet wet. When you go pro, it'll matter a hell of a lot more and I'll make sure you get fights we know are good match-ups.

"When I go pro?"

"Hell yeah. You're going pro eventually. If you want to, that is. You have to want it, or it's not worth it and you won't get very far."

The waitress brings our pie and he digs in like he hasn't eaten in a week.

I just sit there, wondering. Wondering if I want it enough.

The next afternoon, 4:10

I'm holding the heavy bag for Mick while he kicks and punches. Gabe's flipping sandbags while Frankie throws the medicine bag against the wall and Travis does leg curls.

Mick steps back, points at the door. I let go of the bag, turn around.

Erin's there, talking to Travis, who turns and points to me.

I smell the bleach, the sweat, the ugly manliness of it all. I shouldn't be embarrassed but all of a sudden I am.

"Who's that?" Mick asks.

"A friend. I think."

"Alright!" he says. He offers me a high five and I return it. I step past him to meet Erin, who's heading toward me. She's trying to smile but looking nervous and out of place—can't seem to help looking around and shuddering a little.

Mick, Gabe and Travis are all standing there watching me. Well, at her, mostly. She's blushing. My face is hot too.

"Guys, this is Erin." I point at them one by one. "Gabe, Travis, Mick, Frankie."

They all say hi, grinning at me.

Erin nods at them, looks down at her feet.

Gill steps out of the bathroom.

"And that's Gill, the big boss," I say. He gives her a little half-wave.

I reach out to her, get a whiff of the stink from my armpit, and pull my hand back. I pick up a towel from the bench beside us and mop my face while she watches. I suddenly feel like the testosterone-fueled cave man she sees me as.

I should tell her I'll be right back, and go wash up.

No. This is my space, not hers. I didn't ask her to come.

"You want to sit?" I ask, pointing at the bench. "I gotta get something to drink."

She nods, lowers herself halfway to sitting, straightens up to inspect the bench, wipes it off with her hand, then sits. I'm watching her while I grab my water bottle. I sit on the mat a couple of feet in front of her.

"Sorry for the stink."

She tries to smile. "It's okay. It's not too bad."

"Sure it is. I smell like a horse."

She sees I'm smiling and a grin breaks out on her face.

She nods. "Yeah, you do."

The guys have stopped watching us and gone back to training. Frankie's stepped into the cage to take my place with Mick, and I catch Gill checking us out from the other side of the cage.

"What's up?" I ask.

"You missed the first two classes the other day."

"Yeah, so?"

"You haven't missed a class in months. In fact, you haven't even been late. I was wondering if everything was okay."

I snort. "Big deal. So I was a couple of hours late once. That's not why you're here."

She picks at something on the mat, down by her shoe. I look up at the ceiling, waiting to find out what she's up to. Probably wanted to see for herself the place that's turned me into a thug.

She leans toward me, her eyes bright green and focused.

"Why do you fight?" Her voice is sharp, intense.

I knew it. Here it comes. I start to get to my feet, tell her to get out so I can go back to training, but she keeps going.

"I mean, I know about your brother, and it makes sense in a way, since you couldn't wrestle this year. But why "—she looks around the gym—"why this? Is this really you, or just something you have to get out of your system? I mean, I'd understand that. It makes sense."

I start to get up again but she puts her hand on my knee, pushes down.

"Please, just explain it to me, Ross," she says. "I really want to know."

The sounds of the gym fill the space between us—Travis's fists hitting the heavy bag, Gabe's grunts as he hammers out pull-ups, Frankie and Mick's feet padding across the mat while Gill shouts out advice.

Mick takes a shot at Frankie, who blocks it and returns a kick that makes a sharp smack as it hits Mick's thigh.

"Nice one!" Gill shouts.

Mick smiles, steps forward, and he and Frankie exchange a high-five. I laugh.

Erin tilts her head. "Don't they get mad at each other?"

"Not usually. They're not trying to hurt each other—I mean, they are, but not to be mean. They're just pushing each other as hard as they can, to get better. Does that make sense?"

She bites her lip. "Maybe. Kind of. I guess so."

"Look," I say. "Remember when you said wrestlers were so aggressive and treated girls like meat? Not these guys. They don't talk about balling someone or make fun of each other's manhood. They aren't always in a pissing contest to see who's more of a man. I hang around with these guys, I feel good about myself."

She frowns. "Really?"

I point at the ring. "Look."

Gill's in there now, giving Mick a slow-motion demonstration of how to block Frankie and use the opening to shove Frankie into the cage. Mick's taking it all in, asking questions, mimicking Gill's moves. Gill steps back and Mick takes his place. He and Frankie go through the sequence a half-dozen times.

"See? Nothing personal."

She smiles. "I don't think you could convince my mother of that."

"No, probably not."

We watch them for another half minute.

"Think I can convince you of that?"

She waits a second, smiles.

"Probably. I guess you're not so bad."

We sit there a while longer. She's taking it in, wincing a bit with every hit Mick and Frankie lay on each other. But in between, when they joke together, she smiles along. Once in a while she pulls her hair behind her ear and I can see her cheek and neck. I feel like reaching out, taking her hand, but I stink. And I'm not sure what kind of friendship we're working on.

She sighs, slaps my shoulder and stands up.

"I better go. I should be studying Chem right now, and you're supposed to be training."

She holds out her hand and helps me to my feet.

Travis smiles at her as we pass him on the way to the door. She says a quiet "hi" back.

We get to the door and she turns to me and smiles.

"I'm glad I came."

I get into a fighter's stance and pretend to throw a couple of jabs at her gut.

145

"I've got my first real fight Saturday night. Want to come?"

She shakes her head hard. "I'm definitely not ready for that. You'll have to give me time."

I open the door, watch her go. Things could be worse.

Ten minutes later

I'm doing some light sparring with Gabe, hip throws, jiu-jitsu, but not enough to tire me out. I'm feeling loose.

We leave the cage and sit down on the bench together, drink some water and towel off.

"You nervous?" he asks. "You don't seem like it."

"Nah." My head's clear. More clear than I can ever remember.

"How come?"

I shrug. "I don't know."

But I do know. Because Ricky's not in it.

Saturday night, seven o'clock

Gill picks me up from home in his beat-up, rusted pick-up. Mick scoots to the middle and I step in on the passenger side.

I'm worried we're late but try not to show it. The fight's starting right about now and we're a good forty-five minutes away.

Gill looks over and reads my mind.

"Don't worry. You're the last fight of the night," he says. "No sense having too much time to get nervous."

So much for not being nervous.

When he said last week that I was the main event, I figured it had to be a joke. From watching the pro fights at home I know the last one is the highlight: the headline—the guys who are most experienced, who'll put on a better show.

"No joke," Mick said.

"But it's my first fight. How'd that happen?"

Mick pointed a thumb over at Gill.

"Cause you train with him."

An hour and a half later

We pull into the parking lot. It's not exactly what I expect.

A big neon sign sits over the wide front doors. *Lucky Lou's Family Fun Center.* With pictures of a bowling pin, bowling ball, pool cue and eight ball.

I can't believe it. "A bowling alley!"

Mick jabs me in the side with his elbow.

"Welcome to the world of amateur fights."

We go in the front door. It's clean, loud. Ahead is the bowling alley—modern-looking, in good shape, no smoke clouding the air. Gill nudges me to the right. It's a lounge area with a little stand-up sign that says "Reserved: Sundstrom Anniversary Party."

To the left of the lounge entrance is a long hall painted black. At the entrance stand two security guards and a lady behind a little booth. A sign taped to the front of the booth says "General Admission $30. Ring-side seating $50."

Jeez. For an amateur fight, it sure costs enough.

The guard holds out his hand, palm to us. He gestures at me.

"I'll need to see some ID."

"He's one of the fighters," Gill says, and shows the guy our little laminated participant tickets.

The guy looks at it close.

"So you're LeClaire, huh?"

He looks me over like he's sizing up a steak in the grocery store meat aisle.

"Good luck," he says as we walk by, and shakes his head.

The music and crowd noise grows as we walk down the hall, and I can see more and more of the cage right in front of us. I feel myself getting jacked up a bit, excited. Then we come out into a decent-sized room. It's half-dark, music's playing over a crappy sound system. There's a row of chairs around the cage. The rest of the room is packed with people standing around, beers and plastic cups of alcohol in their hands. It's not as rough a crowd as I expected—a lot of twenty-somethings in leather jackets and dark jeans and styled hair. The bar area's to the right at the back of the room, raised up on a large platform. It's packed with people too.

We walk along the left wall to the back corner, squeezing past people between us and the cage.

The cage is smaller than I expected. I point it out to Mick.

"Yeah," he yells over the music and crowd. "It's good when you go to the bigger size. It lets you plan better. There's more space to strategize. This size, the fights are usually over quicker. It's more intense, actually."

A couple of guys are going at it. They're quick and hitting each other hard. When Gill said I'd be the main fight of the evening, I figured the rest of the guys would be hacks training at places like the Jong-Qi Judo club back home in Rosslyn. But these two guys, at least, are pretty good. They're taking it to each other on the feet, bobbing and weaving, attacking and countering, mixing it up good. Then one of them rushes, gets the other in the clinch, forces him against the cage, trips him to the ground, and postures up.

"Man, they know their stuff," I say out loud.

Gill pushes me past, to the corner, and turns me to face him.

"Don't worry." He slaps my check gently. "Look at me. Remember. This fight's not about them. It's not even really about your opponent." He thumps me in the forehead. "It's all you. You've got the skills you've got. Now you just have to use them. Clear your head, read the situation, attack and react."

A tall, dark-haired guy in a sport jacket and jeans spots us from a table behind the cage, waves, and pushes past the fighters and hangers-on between him and us. He walks up with his hand reached out to Gill.

"Gill Sans? Rob Lank. Really good to meet you. Really good," he says, pumping Gill's hand the whole time.

He smacks me on the shoulder.

"And this must be your fighter. Rick?"

"Ross," I say.

"Ross. Yeah. Well, like I said, good to have you here. A real honor. But hey, listen. We've got a little ... situation."

My guts tighten.

"What kind of situation?" Gill growls.

The promoter coughs nervously.

"Well, it looks like the other guy's info was wrong. He's coming in heavy."

Gill's starting to get tense.

"Heavy?"

A bead of sweat is rolling down the guy's forehead now.

"Uh, like, one-ninety."

Gill's immediately furious.

"One-ninety! That's not even close to welterweight!"

He scans the people behind the cage.

"That him?"

He points at a guy a good three inches taller than everyone around him. Muscles pop out of his t-shirt like sausages and I'm all of sudden glad I didn't bother trying to cut weight. Tattoos cover his entire chest and both shoulders, with a neck as thick as his giant head. He looks about twenty, twenty-five years old.

Gill grabs the promoter by the collar of his sports jacket.

"If he's one-ninety, I'm anorexic!"

He turns to me.

"We're going."

It feels like my guts are going to bust out of my chest.

"What do you mean?" I cry out.

Mick jumps in.

"I know that guy. I've seen him fight. Pro."

Gill smacks his fist into his palm.

"And?" I ask.

Mick grimaces. "He lost, but not before breaking the other guy's nose. He's one serious mofo."

Gill whirls on the promoter, almost pounces him.

"You dirty--"

The promoter flinches, leans away. "Look, I wouldn't have put the fight together if I knew ahead of time –"

"Forget it!" Gill says. "No way I'm letting my kid in the ring with a guy like that."

The promoter looks like he's been hit by a semi. He grabs Gill by the shoulders. "You can't do that. It's the headline fight –"

Gill throws the guys arms off him. "I just did."

I push up between them, face Gill. I should be scared, but right now all I feel is wired up to fight.

"I'll do it anyway. I don't care."

"No way, kid," Gill says. "You're not up to it. You'll get your ass kicked." He glares at the promoter as he says it. "I don't want to be responsible for you getting damaged."

"What the hell's that supposed to mean?" He's got me going now. I look back at the big dude. "You don't know I'll lose. There's no way you could know that. Give me some credit. Besides, it's my ass, not yours."

Gill squints, chews on his tongue, looks everywhere but at me. He's pumping up and down on his feet like he's about to explode. Finally, he turns to the promoter, pokes the guy so hard he stumbles backward.

"If I find you set this thing up on purpose, you better find a good place to hide," he says between gritted teeth.

The guy stays a step back. He manages to smile a bit.

"Th – thanks. You're ... thanks." He turns and pushes his way back through the crowd. My opponent must have figured out I was still in, because he gives me a grin from across the room—the kind that Ricky used to give. The one that says he's going to enjoy looking down on my smashed body.

Twenty minutes later

I'm in the corner of the room, sitting on a plastic chair with a cracked seat. Mick's been holding the pads while I did some light boxing, left-right-knee combinations, that kind of thing. Now Gill's massaging my arms, telling me to loosen up.

It's all just like Ricky. Just like that match with Sorenson. I'm being set up for a loss, and I know it. We all know it.

If Gill's still mad or worried, it doesn't show. He's all business. Mick's not done trying to get me to quit, though.

"You can still walk away, buddy. It's just one fight. We can get you another one in a few weeks. Right, Gill?"

Gill nods grimly.

"There's no shame in letting this one go," Mick continues. "It isn't worth getting yourself stomped into the mat this early in your training. This could go very, very bad."

I grin. "Worse than the shark tank?"

Mick tries to smile but can't quite pull it off.

"If you were in my shoes, would you back out?" I ask Gill.

He looks away. Then he shakes his head.

"Would you?" I ask Mick.

He snorts. "Probably not."

They look at each other. Gill shrugs and stands up. I watch him walk over to the promoter but can't hear what he's saying. The promoter's face turns a bit gray and he nods. Gill walks back to me, calm.

"What'd you tell him?" I ask.

Gill shrugs. "I said if the ref accidentally makes any bad calls in the other guy's favor, all three of them'll have a hard time going to the bathroom tomorrow morning."

He kneels down in front of me again.

"Remember the most important thing, right?"

I know exactly what he's thinking. "Fight as mean as I can, but don't fight angry."

He stands up, nods, grins.

"And, there's nothing wrong with losing," I add.

He shakes his head, slaps me on the cheek.

"No way you're going to lose."

Fifteen minutes later

The last fight ends with one guy slumped on the floor against the cage, his face looking like it was put through a juicer, and the other guy jumping up and down like he just won the lottery. Mick and I've been going through slow-motion clinches and throws, talking out the moves. The whole time I'm repeating Gill's words in my head. *I'm not going to lose. I'm not going to lose.*

The promoter steps into the ring, announces that we've reached the final fight of the night, that the first fighter is from Rosslyn, Minnesota and makes my name stretch out for thirty seconds as he yells it through the mic.

"Ryannnnn ... Six Gunnnnnn .... LeClaire!"

Me and Mick look at each other.

"Six gun?" I say. "Where'd he come up with that one?"

Mick grins. "We'll have to work on getting you a real label."

I step up to the ref, who checks my hand wraps and finger nails. Then a guy greases my face with Vaseline.

I walk up the little metal steps into the ring. It's small, tight. There's a few hundred people on the other side of the fence, and it feels like I'm in a police interrogation with a light glaring into my face. Half of them aren't even looking at me, but a bunch are pointing and talking to each other. It's obvi-

153

ous from the looks on their faces that they aren't betting any money on me.

I stand against the cage wall trying to relax, bounce a little on my feet, avoid the adrenalin dump as much as I can. Hit my fist into my palm, throw a couple of punches, bend down at the knees and back up a few times. I didn't imagine it'd feel this awkward.

Meanwhile, the promoter's announcing the other guy— "Jasonnnnn... The Anaconnnnnda... Giffffford." Heavy music blares while the other guy goes through the same routine with the ref and the grease man.

I take a few deep breaths, think through the moves we've worked on over and over, imagine him getting kicked down, knocked out, submitted. *You're not going to lose. You're not going to lose. You're not going to lose.*

The other guy's stepping into the ring. He raises his arms, struts around a couple of times, and a wall of cheers hits us. The hometown boy. Behind me I hear someone say "This'll be a bloodbath, dude"—and not like that was a bad thing.

The ring girl comes in holding up a square sign with the number 1 on it, wearing not near enough clothing, and what she's got on is six sizes too tight. The crowd—at least, the guys in the crowd—hoot as she takes a turn around the ring. She looks as nervous and awkward as I do.

The ref steps between me and the Beast, holds his hands out to the side, looks to the other guy, then to me.

"You sure you want to do this?" he asks me.

I give him a look that I hope says "screw off."

He shakes his head.

"Alright."

He steps back as he pulls his arms in.

"Go to it!" he shouts.

Three minutes later

I'm slumped back on the plastic chair, more battered than winded. The last three minutes are a blur. It felt like thirty seconds.

The smaller cage threw me for a loop. There was less room to step away, plan anything out. And the guy's a maniac. He came at me like a 200-pound bullet, bashing me with a quick looping right to the head. That got an equal amount of groans and cheers from the crowd. Then as I stumbled backwards, he slammed me against the cage and started giving me shots to the ribs. I could hear Gill's screamed instructions, just barely over the crowd's shouts.

"Get out of there! Get out!"

I pushed my hands under his armpits and spun back into the middle of the ring.

He rushed me again, but I danced to the side, just like we practiced, and hit him a glancing blow to the side of the head. Not enough to do any damage, but it got his attention.

He whipped back around and we squared off. Then a stutter-step forward, and his fist hit just above my eye. Then another to the opposite cheek.

Gill was shouting. "Fists up! Block! Counter!"

In the gap between the guy's right hand and his body, I threw a decent uppercut that made solid contact with his chin.

He hardly flinched, though, and came at me again. I danced back, ducking under his blows, and shot to get a leg. He sprawled backward almost instantly. Just like Gabe had done a hundred times before. I shoved myself lower and under him while he dragged me backwards until he was against the fence. His fists

155

curled around underneath my arm and hammered into my face. I could feel the blows jolting my head but it was like it was happening to someone else. All I knew was that leg, the one I had to pull down. Then I snagged his other ankle and he settled onto his butt with a whump that got me a cheer from the crowd.

I jumped on him but he was so huge he just shoved me off and to the side.

Immediately he was on me, but I managed to wrap my legs around his waist in half-guard. He smothered me, put his hands in my face, shoved off, and brought down an elbow. The crowd groaned and I saw blood splattered on his forearm—my blood. He brought down a couple more blows.

"Defend yourself!" The ref shouted. I put up my arms to block him, tried to grab his wrists to control him. It slowed down the punches and elbows, but only a little. If the bell hadn't rung, the fight would've been over.

Gill shoves a water bottle into my mouth while the cut man uses a q-tip to stop the blood gushing out of a cut above my nose between the eyebrows.

I take a swig.

"Breathe easy," he says. "Slow your breathing. Now listen to me. You gotta use his weight against him. When he comes at you, dance away. Feint a shot to the body, then jab into his face and get out of there. And go for a leg kick to keep him guessing. Got that? Dance, feint, find the opening, leg-kick. Got it?"

I nod, trying to pay attention and hoping my head'll clear.

The girl walks the ring, card held high. Round two.

The bell rings. The ref gestures at me. "Get up. Get up."

Gill pushes me to my feet and into the ring.

"Go to it, kid!"

Round 2

As the ref steps out of the way, the guy charges again. I do like Gill says—dance backward just out of his reach, bob to the side, then as he shoots past me I plant my foot, lean in and give him a fist right to the face. He stumbles, twisting around, and I follow up with a looping left that catches his chin. The crowd roars and I feel the adrenalin kick in again.

We face off. This time, he's in his stance, cautious. He steps forward, peppers me with a couple of right jabs that I easily duck away from. He comes at me again, the same thing, and I whip out a right leg kick that smacks into his thigh.

The crowd reacts and I can hear Mick's voice mixed in, shouting encouragement. I can't help smiling.

The guy growls and lunges forward, swinging for the fences. My hands are up and I deflect the blow aimed at the left side. His right hand comes at me and I lean back. Then I feel it—an immediate stabbing pain as his finger pokes into my eye. Without thinking my hands come over it. I feel the shot to my ribs and stagger back.

"Time! Time!" the ref shouts, and steps between us as the crowd boos.

He puts his hands on my shoulders. "You okay?"

It feels like there's a knife stuck between my eyeball and the socket. I bend over, head in my hands.

"Can you fight?" the ref shouts.

I don't answer. I'm back on the wrestling mat with Matt Sorenson, back in the basement with Ricky grinding at my eye.

"Can you fight?"

The anger's hovering over me, ready to knife into me, make

me want to maim the guy any way I can. But I'm not on the wrestling mat, and I'm not in the basement, and this guy isn't Ricky or Sorenson.

I raise my head, my right hand still over my eye, and nod.

"You sure?" he says.

I nod, walk away, squeeze my eye shut and open a few times. I'm near Gill and Mick now, hear them yelling at me to pull out if I have to.

I take my hand off my eye, blink a few times. It's still bleary and hurts like hell, but I get into my stance.

"You sure?" the ref asks. I raise my hands a bit more, nod to the ref while looking at my opponent. The Beast gives a lopsided half-grin and we step forward, touch gloves.

If I thought he'd go easy on me after nearly taking my eye out, I was wrong. He rushes me again, gets his hands under my armpits, and tries to throw me sideways. I keep my balance but he has me against the cage, shoving me, making it almost impossible to breathe.

"How's that eye?" he sneers. Then he hits me with a right to the ribs.

With a surge of anger I shove back at him and spin out, hitting him with an elbow as I step away.

Then I charge. It's stupid. I know it. In a second, he's pulled his arm back and plowed me straight in the face. I stumble backward, barely stay on my feet.

As I struggle back upright he jumps forward and plows me again—this time, a right hook and left hook. I fall to the left, barely avoiding another right hook. My left hand goes down to stop me and I stumble sideways, away from him.

He bears down on my again, his eyes hungry for blood.

Something kicks in and before he can step into me, I plant a leg and let go a kick straight to his head.

The crowd roars. He falls to the side. I jump forward, slam a left knee into his face, and the crowd roars again.

I jump on him, get him to his back, get into half guard, and quick as lighting stuff a couple of shots into his gut, then an elbow to his head. But he rolls into me, gets on top.

I know this is trouble. I'm about to get mashed into the mat.

He raises his right fist up past his head, ready to bring it down.

But the bell rings and the ref's got his hands between us, pushing the guy off me. Saved again.

I get up and we bump into each other on the way to our corners.

"You're dead," he says.

Gill's got me right away, helping me down onto the chair, toweling me off, shoving the water bottle into my hand.

"Breathe! Breathe!"

"Kid! You're the man!" Mick yells from the other side of the fence. "You're taking it to him!"

"Am I doing okay?" I ask Gill between gasps.

He bends down in front of me, rubbing first one arm and then the other to loosen me up.

"You're doing amazing."

He moves to my shoulder, massages them.

"What do I do?" I gasp. "He's going to win, isn't he?"

"You might've taken that round," Gill says. "Hard to say. You take it to him like that again, you could steal it. Just do more of the same thing. Keep out of his reach. Don't try to get him to the ground—he's too big. He's not throwing any kicks and he's not going for takedowns. Just keep away from his punches and keep countering. Dodge and counter. Can you do that?"

"Yeah. Yeah."

The bell rings.

"Back in! Back in!" the ref yells.

Gill pulls me to my feet and slaps a hand against my cheek.

"And remember. Don't fight angry. Got it?"

I take a deep breath, lean my head to the right shoulder and then the left.

"Got it."

Round 3

As we square off again and he charges and I dance away, a strange thing happens. I'm in the fight, dodging and countering and getting hit by a couple of shots but still mostly avoiding damage. One part of me is hearing the crowd and behind it somehow I'm going through the sparring and grappling routines with the guys at Top Form.

Part of me knows I'm one solid punch away from being laid out cold but pictures are popping into my mind in the middle and around and over top everything. Coach telling me I'm kicked off the team and trying to talk to Erin on Christmas Eve and Mom making pancakes and Erin's mom in the grocery store and Ricky coming through the door with his duffel bag and stupid sneering face.

Anaconda hits me full-force in the gut and I double over, spinning away and trying to stay out of his reach. Gill and Mick are yelling at me to keep my hands up and counter but at the same time I'm back in our house, I'm six years old, and Dad's with me on the couch reading me the user manual for his new table saw.

And it's all good.

Anaconda's face is bloated red. I can tell he's running on empty as he staggers toward me. I step backward. Gill's voice comes through—"Keep your hands up!" I lift them, but they're back down at my chest and he yells it again and I lift them again and they fall and I realize I'm gassed just like the other guy.

He takes a swing with his right and somehow I manage to lean away from it. He takes another and it clips my shoulder. He follows it with a left and I duck under it, more of a fall than a duck. But he put too much into it and lurches past me, bending over. Without even thinking I pivot on my right foot, swing over him, and jump on his back.

"Put your hooks in!" Gill and Mick are screaming, over and over. I clamp my legs around his back on both sides, stick my right arm partway under his chin. He grabs around behind his head, yanking at me, but I'm clinched too tight on him, he can't shake me. My left arm yanks back on his forehead and the right snakes under the chin, tight. I pull and pull with every bit of energy I have left. My arms feel like lead, they can't hold much longer. He's stumbling around the ring, and he's clawing at my arms to pull them loose.

Just a few more seconds. I can feel it. He's about to tap. Or pass out.

I hear the crowd roaring and Gill and Mick screaming at me to hold on, and it's coming.

Then with one final shot of pure rage he jumps up and arches his back. I feel us sailing backward. know what's coming. I slam into the mat, his two hundred pounds on top of me, crushing

161

me. My breath is gone, my hands slip off him. Then in one quick move he rolls, throwing me over with him, gets my back, and sinks his arm under one armpit and against my neck, his hand hooked around his other wrist. I know this feeling, know what's coming.

Gill's practically screaming. "Tap! Tap!"

There's no way out. I can feel myself about to go unconscious. Then I feel my fingers tapping against his leg.

The ref jumps in, pulls the guy off me. I roll to my back, knees bent upward, completely spent, sucking in hard gallons of air.

The whole world is full of yelling and cheering around me. I turn my head to the side and see Anaconda's feet and knees racing around the ring, jumping up and down. I look higher, he's grinning, hands in the air.

Gill's leaning over me, holding a hand out. I grab on and he pulls me to a sitting position.

The crowd roars more.

I take a few more breaths, he claps me on the back with his free hand, not letting go of the other.

"You ready?"

I nod and he pulls, and I stagger to my feet

The crowd roars even more.

I look over at Anaconda, wishing I was him.

Mick's beside me, thumping me on my back, then hugging me and lifting me off my feet, whirling me around.

"You did it, buddy!"

Didn't he notice?

"I tapped! He choked me out! I lost!"

He puts me down, raises my fist in the air. The crowd roars again.

"Hear that?" he says.

I look over at Gill's grinning face.

"He should've killed you," Mick says. "You should be on a stretcher right now."

I'm so beat up I can barely stand. My cheek and nose and ribs are killing me. But Anaconda doesn't look much better. There's a goose egg on his forehead so big it looks like it'll pop any second, and one eye is swollen shut. His left thigh is covered with a map of welts from where I kicked him over and over.

The promoter walks up.

"That was a hell of a fight, kid. A hell of a fight."

Then he turns to Anaconda and announces the win while Gill helps me out of the cage.

Ten minutes later

The medic's leaning over me, examining the cut over my eye. Past his shoulder I see Mick looking at me, concerned.

I smile.

"Tell me I'm still beautiful," I say, and try to wink. My eye's so puffed up it's already mostly shut.

Gill gives me a slug to the shoulder.

"It looks like you'll be missing a couple of days of school again, champ."

I nod, then look up and smile.

"So I'll see you Monday morning?"

He tilts his head, searches my face like he's wondering if I'm all the way crazy or only half. Then he smiles and smacks me on the shoulder.

"Sure. But just to watch."